Books by Michael Lister

(John Jordan Novels)
Power in the Blood
Blood of the Lamb
Flesh and Blood
The Body and the Blood
Blood Sacrifice
Rivers to Blood
Innocent Blood
Blood Money
Blood Moon

(Short Story Collections)
North Florida Noir
Florida Heat Wave
Delta Blues
Another Quiet Night in Desparation

(Remington James Novels)
Double Exposure
Separation Anxiety

(Merrick McKnight Novels)
Thunder Beach
A Certain Retribution

(Jimmy "Soldier" Riley Novels)
The Big Goodbye
The Big Beyond
The Big Hello
The Big Bout

(Sam Michaels and Daniel Davis Series)
Burnt Offerings
Separation Anxiety

BLOOD MOON

a John Jordan Mystery

by Michael Lister

M

Pulpwood Press
Panama City, FL

Inquiries should be addressed to:
Pulpwood Press
P.O. Box 35038
Panama City, FL 32412

Lister, Michael.
Blood Moon / Michael
Lister.
-----1st ed.
p. cm.

ISBN: 978-1-888146-55-4   Hardcover

ISBN: 978-1-888146-56-1   Paperback

Book Design by Adam Ake

Printed in the United States

1 3 5 7 9 10 8 6 4 2

First Edition

For Lou Columbus

For 1492 and the discovery of a great collaborator and an even better friend.

Thanks for your gentle, egoless, insightful input and inspiration, the amazing images you capture, and the great conversations about things that really matter.

Thank You

Dawn Lister, Jill Mueller, Lou Columbus,
Mike Harrison, Dayton Lister, Phillip Weeks,
Michael Connelly, Adam Ake, Jeff Moore,
Aaron Bearden, Dave Lloyd, Dan Finley, Tony
Simmons, Emily Balazs, Charlene Childers

Chapter One

Waiting.

Alone in the dark.

Thinking.

Praying.

Preparing.

Waiting.

I was waiting for a call—the single most important phone call of my life.

Earlier in the night I had arrived home to find Anna gone.

Not just gone. Taken.

I had found our solitary trailer in the Prairie Palm Mobile Home Community Phase II trashed, all its lights on, the front door flung open, and both Anna's and her soon-to-be ex-husband Chris Taunton's cars in the yard.

I had quickly searched everywhere. The trailer. The yard. The vehicles. Down by the river.

Then a number I didn't recognize appeared on my phone and a voice said, "I have your wife."

And everything changed.

The voice was unrecognizable to me. I just knew it wasn't Chris.

The caller had referred to Anna as my wife. Could

mean he didn't know us very well—or that he wasn't being literal.

I had been thinking about it. What would someone close to us or who knew us well call us? Not husband and wife. *I have your girlfriend. I have your friend. I have Anna.* Chris and anyone sympathetic to him would call her *his* wife. They'd call me the son of a bitch trying to steal her away from him. Was he really going to kill Chris? Was there anything I could do? I'd try again to stop him when he called back.

The truth was no one had come up with a name for what Anna was to me, but I couldn't help but think him calling her my wife was significant.

"She is safe," he had said. "She is fine. But if you contact the authorities, she is dead. If you tell anyone—anyone at all—she is dead. If you do not do exactly what I say when I say, she is dead."

I hadn't responded.

"Do you understand?" he'd asked.

"I do."

"Thank you for not making ridiculous threats and absurd proclamations. You are wise. This is going to run very smoothly. You do what I say when I say and you'll have her back safe and sound very soon."

I had then asked to speak to her.

"When I call back," he'd said. "When I have her situated. For now I just wanted to make sure you didn't contact anyone before you knew exactly what was going on."

"I won't call anyone," I'd said.

"I have her ex-husband too. He came up as we were leaving and tried to be a hero. He will turn up dead in the next day or so. It will appear to be suicide. You will know what I am capable of."

"I only care about Anna," I'd said. "Do what you want to with Chris, but there's no need to kill him to convince me of anything. I'm convinced."

I wasn't sure if that was enough to save Chris's life, but I wasn't sure there was much more I could do.

"I'll do anything to get her back," I'd said.

"That's what I'm counting on."

There was so much more I had wanted to say, but I knew better.

"I'll call back soon," he'd said. "Be ready."

Since then I had been waiting for the call and readying myself.

Sitting here in the dark, in the single chair in the single wide, going deep inside, distancing myself from everything—including Anna. Especially Anna. If I let myself think about what she meant to me, let myself consider what would happen if I failed, I'd get her killed.

I could hear myself breathing. Slow, continuous, rhythmic inhalation and exhalation. My relative silence revealing all the sounds that normally go unnoticed.

Around me, the mobile home creaked and groaned. Beyond the thin paneling, old insulation, and aging, faded aluminum, the nocturnal noises of the September night were loud and could be heard as if nothing were between us.

A lonely, whistling wind.

The buzz and hum, thump and saw, chirp and croak of reptiles, animals, and insects.

The gurgle and bubble of the Apalachicola River as it wound its way toward the bay.

Somewhere in the distance, a diesel engine laboring to pull its load and a dog barking desultorily.

There were lockers inside me—all-black barrack

storage lockers—and in them I locked away all but the essentials, all feelings, all sentiment, all fear and what-ifs, all but rudimentary humanity.

In the underground bunker that was now my mind, everything that wasn't essential to getting Anna back, which included my feelings for her and the compassion and empathy, civility and humanity I ordinarily went to such great lengths to cultivate, was tucked away, locked up tight, in something darker than darkness, where even lost light had been vanquished.

Stillness.

Self-containment.

Self-control.

Self-reliance.

I was something I hadn't been in a long time—a soldier awaiting orders, a mercenary concerned only with the mission.

Most of me didn't like being this way. Part of me liked it too much.

The truth was I wasn't as good at it as I had once been—something I saw as a sign of growth. Something I hoped wouldn't cost Anna her life. I had spent years nurturing a life of connection and compassion, of humanity and soul—all of which had led to an integration that made it more difficult to disintegrate or compartmentalize.

The phone rang then, its small screen bright in the dark room, and the waiting was over.

Chapter Two

"Hello."

My throat was dry, my voice small and sleepy sounding.

"Did I wake you?" he asked, his voice tinged with sarcasm and surprise.

"No."

"Have you done anything stupid?" he asked.

"No."

"I certainly hope that is the case."

"It is."

"You should know . . . I am not a bad man. I am, however, a desperate one. I have no desire to harm the girl in any way. And I won't. Not as long as you do exactly as I tell you."

"I will."

"If you do not, her blood is on your hands."

I didn't say anything.

"I have studied you," he said. "I know you. I know what you are capable of. I am not going to ask you to do anything you can't do. I am not going to ask you to do anything you would not be willing to do to get your wife back. You are smart. Very smart. Do not let that make you believe you can outsmart me on this. Under other circumstances, maybe, but not this. And if you even try . . ."

"I won't. I just want Anna back. Nothing else matters to me."

"I am going to let you speak to her. This is an act of good faith. Do not abuse it. The purpose is to let you know she is as I say. Nothing else. She can tell you nothing apart from her condition. She has been blindfolded from the moment she regained consciousness. She has seen nothing. She knows nothing. If she did, she would not be talking to you. Understand?"

"I understand," I said.

"Oh, and I will be listening to everything that is said."

"John?" Anna said.

"I love you. Are you okay?"

"I'm fine. Honestly. I'm blindfolded. They used chloroform on me. But I haven't been mistreated."

"When we were kids I gave you something to show our support for Atlanta during the child murders. What was it?"

"A green ribbon."

"I'm going to do exactly what he asks," I said. "Gonna get you back safe and sound."

"I know."

"I'm sorry I let this happen."

"Listen," she said, "I need to tell you something. I know you know it, but I want you to hear me say it again. The only regret I have, I'll ever have, is not being with you sooner. I love you with all of me. And no matter what happens, it's not your fault and I wouldn't trade a single moment I got with you."

"You're gonna get many, many more. Just do what he tells you. We'll be back together very soon."

"Okay," the man's voice said.

"I love you," she said.

"I love you so much."

"So you see," he said. "She is fine. And she will stay that way. Just help a desperate man out and I swear to you everything will work out. You two will get a happy ending after all."

"Tell me what to do."

"Hide the idiot's car."

"Speaking of the idiot," I said. "Don't kill him. There's no need. I'm going to do exactly what you say. Killing him would just—"

"It's already done. Now listen—and don't interrupt me again. Go to work in the morning. Tell Anna's boss she is having severe morning sickness and will not be able to work for a while—probably no more than a few days. Nothing to worry about. The baby is fine. She just can't get out of bed. Follow your normal routine. Act ordinary. Don't talk to anyone about any of this. I am not alone in this. I have people watching you, listening to you. We will know if you say or do anything."

"I've already told you—I won't."

"Make sure tomorrow is the most normal day ever. Do this. Nothing more. We will be watching."

"Then what?" I asked.

"Then I will call you and tell you what to do next."

"That's it?"

"That's it."

"You're not going to tell me what I have to do to get Anna back?"

"I've told you the first thing you have to do.

Remember John, one day at a time."

"How long will everything take?"

"No more time than Jonah was in the belly of the big fish."

"How will I get her back?"

"By doing exactly as I say."

"I want to know you have a plan to get her back to me, that you really are going to do as you've said you will."

"We're going to meet. Before this is over you're going to have something I want very badly. And we're going to make an exchange. It's all very simple. Now get some rest and be ready. And no more questions. Just listen to instructions and follow them from here on out. I won't tell you again."

"You won't have to," I said, and we ended the call.

Chapter Three

The moon was immense and magnificent, making the earth below look luminous.

Stepping out into my front yard to move Chris's car, I stopped, transfixed by the translucent quality of the leaves on the trees.

Gazing up, I took in the radiant night all around me.
Breathe.

Three slow, deep breaths.

In . . . and . . . out.

In . . . and . . . out.

In . . . and . . . out.

Now back to the task at hand.

Chris's keys weren't in his car.

I considered my options as I scoured the area to see if he might have dropped them.

You could get it towed.

That'd draw too much attention to it.

True. How about—

I found the keys on the ground near the front door next to the wooden steps.

Since I had no neighbors and wasn't expecting any company anytime soon, I decided to pull the car around back, parking it behind the trailer in a small stand of cypress trees that mostly concealed it.

Sorry I couldn't do more for you. I would not have had you go out the way you did. Thanks for anything you did to try to save Anna.

Back inside, back in the dark, I returned to the chair to resume replaying my conversation with Anna's abductor in my mind.

His voice made him sound younger than I would've expected. Not juvenile exactly, but quite young. And it had very little discernible accent—like someone from the area who had put in some effort to eliminate much of its regionality.

There was something about the quality of his voice that elicited trust—a veracity that made it seem as though he were earnest and honest.

He spoke in a formal manner for the most part, using very few contractions, speaking slowly and carefully. But it was inconsistent. A few times he slipped into a more informal quick response repartee.

Was he just nervous?

Was everything an affect or were the more formal exchanges the more real and revealing?

Maybe he had prepared some of what he said ahead of time—perhaps he even wrote it down—while at other times, in order to respond to what I was saying, he had to go off script, improvise.

He seemed to know a good bit about me, but I still wondered about him calling Anna my wife. Was he just not being literal? Was he doing it as a way of emphasizing what he had done, or planned to do, to Chris?

He wanted me to do something I'd be willing to do to get Anna back. But it had to be something I wasn't just willing but able to do. Was it something I was in a unique position for or uniquely qualified to do? Or was I just random, convenient, wrong place wrong time?

I'd know soon enough. It was a waste of mental energy to try to figure it out now.

I had been able to discern no background noises. Had they been there and I just hadn't been able to hear them, or was he more professional than his youngish voice would suggest and he ensured there were none?

Was he a professional? Just hired to do a job? Or did

he have a personal stake in this? It was hard to tell from the conversation. I knew what he'd said, but wasn't sure I bought it. He seemed somewhat dispassionate at times, but knew so much and seemed fully engaged.

Questions without answers. I was used to that.

Answers would come—or they wouldn't. Only one really mattered. Would I be able to save Anna?

Chapter Four

She had been so happy. Even with Chris calling to say he was coming over to talk. Even with his child inside her. Even with all the challenges, all the slings and arrows, all the issues to be faced. They were facing them together. She and John were together.

A noise at the door.

She knew John would be home soon.

Not afraid of Chris. Not afraid of anything.

Opening the door.

Not Chris. Small guy. Ski mask. Something in his hand.

Turning. Starting to run. Someone behind her.

Turning back. Toward the small guy. Shoving him.

Chris pulling up. Honking his horn. Yelling at the men.

"What the—" one man was saying.

"Who the fuck is that?"

"Not sure. Not John. Come on."

Grabbed from behind. Something at her mouth.

Chris running toward them. Something in his hand. A bat?

Struggling against the strong man. The small man pulling a gun on Chris. Shooting. Chris hit. Down.

Can't resist any longer. Deep inhalation. Then nothing.

W*aking later.*

Blindfolded.

Bumpy ride. Back of van bouncing down a dirt road.

Chris whispering, "I'm gonna get you out of this. I swear."

"Are you okay? You shot?"

"Yeah. So it may be the last thing I do, but I'm gonna get you out of this, away from them. What's this about? Why're they doing this?"

"No idea. But don't do anything yet. Wait to see what—"

"Not now. When they stop to get us out."

Time passing.

Listening to the sounds of the road. Trying to figure out where they are, where they're taking them.

Highway. No traffic. No stopping.

Seams of a short bridge.

Slowing. Turning onto a dirt road.

Chris sounding bad beside her.

"I'm sorry for everything," he whispers. "I just got caught up in some stupid, selfish stuff."

Nodding. Not saying anything.

"I love you, Anna. Always have. Always will."

Van slowing. Squeaking breaks. Stopping.

Doors opening.

Chris lunging. Yelling.

Bodies hitting the ground. Rolling. Gasping. Groaning. Punches. Thwacks and thuds. Slaps. Heaving breathing.

Someone yelling for help.

Fast, heavy footfalls. Running. Kicking. Moans.

Loud gunshot blast.

Then nothing.

Chapter Five

Morning.

Daybreak.

Soft pink glow growing beyond the slash pines along the eastern horizon.

Phone. Shattered silence.

It was Dad.

"Did you shoot Chris Taunton?" he asked.

"I did not. Why do you ask?"

"He's in Bay Medical in bad shape. Been shot."

"He's alive?"

"Barely. That surprise you? What's going on?"

"What did he say?"

"Says it was an accident, that he did it to himself while cleaning his gun, but it *is not* a self-inflicted wound, and he's asking to see you."

My first thought was that Chris was dead.

My second was if he wasn't, he soon would be.

Sallow skin stretched over skull-like dried-out cigar paper. Matted, tangled, oil-tinged hair. Dark stubble. Dirty, blood-stained face. Erratic, labored breathing.

When he blinked his small, inky eyes partially open, he looked worse. Bloodshot. Unfocused. Jaundiced.

When he finally recognized me, he strained to open the tiny moist marbles all the way as anger transformed his tear-streaked face, contorting his parchment-thin skin.

"What . . . the . . . hell . . . have you done?" he managed to push out in airy, harsh whispers.

"What do you know?" I asked. "What can you tell me?"

"Why . . ." he said, then trailed off, taking a moment to regroup.

"Take your time," I said. "Use your energy for communicating rather than anger."

"Why . . . are . . . they . . . doing this?"

I shook my head. "I don't know yet."

"Who . . . are . . . they?"

"I—"

"What . . . did . . . you . . . do . . . to them?"

"I don't know anything yet," I said. "Except they want me to do something—get something to trade for Anna."

"If . . . any . . . thing . . . happ . . . ens . . . to her," he slowly, breathily hissed, "I . . . will . . . kill . . . you. Swear on her . . . life . . . I . . . will. *On . . . her . . . life.*"

"What can you tell me about them? What did you see? Hear? How are they treating her?"

He shook his head slowly, dislodging more tears that snaked down his soiled face.

"Not . . . much. Seem . . . sort of . . . professional . . . Like amateurs . . . taking . . . a pro . . . fess . . . ional . . . approach. Two guys. One . . . young . . . dark hair . . . skin . . . eyes. Not . . . black, but . . . dark." He shook his head. "Got . . . nothin' . . . on the other. Rough . . . with me. Not

... with her. But ... doesn't ... mean ... they won't ...
be."

I nodded and tried not to think about that.

"Do ... what they ... say ... goddamnit. Don't ...
try too ... hard ... to be ... too smart. Get ... her back.
I'd ... rather her ... be alive with ... you ... than ..."

I nodded again and indicated something with my
eyes—appreciation, maybe. Or solidarity. Or understanding.

"Are ... we ... only ones ... who know?" he asked.

"Think so."

"Let ... me ... help ... if I ... can."

"Okay," I said, nodding.

Something flickered in his eyes and they widened
momentarily the way eyes do when the mind has an *aha*
moment.

"They ... think I'm ... dead," he said. "Leave ...
it that ... way. Get ... your dad to ... put me under ...
different name. Best ... for Anna ... they think ... I'm
dead. Maybe ... I can help with ..."

"I'll see what I can do," I said.

He nodded and we were quiet a moment.

"I ..." he began, "... hate you ... so ... fuckin' ...
much. And ... the life of ... only person ... I've ever
loved is in ... your hands. I ... I ... don't know ... what to
do ... with that."

"Nothin' to do," I said.

"Meant ... what I ... said. Fuck this ... up ... and I
... will ... kill ... you."

"Assuming you're still alive yourself," I said.

"I'll ... stay ... alive ... just to do ... it."

"I need your trust," I said to Dad.

"You've got it. You know that."

We were standing in the ICU hallway right outside Chris's room. Activity around us. Nurses at the large station in the center of the ward, others in and out of rooms. Guests, two at a time, entering and exiting the rooms of loved ones. An occasional doctor. A two-person cleaning crew in light burgundy scrubs slowly making their way around the unit. None of it quiet. None of it particularly careful.

"I need your blind trust."

"Okay. You've earned it. Thousand times at least."

I thought about how true that statement really was. I had proven myself over and over to this man in a variety of situations and circumstances over the course of several decades. He knew I'd keep my word and do the very best I could to do the right and honorable thing.

"I'll tell you everything when I can, but until then . . ."

He nodded.

"Can you put out a release saying Chris died from a gunshot wound, then put him under a different name?"

"He still in danger?"

"No questions. Not yet."

He nodded again. "Okay. Done."

Chapter Six

Work.

Normal routine.

Acting as if my entire world was not being held hostage for an as yet unknown ransom.

Stopped at the front gate. Called over to the window by the sergeant—a young guy with short, dark blond hair, bright blue eyes, and bright white teeth almost always on display in his kind, infectious smiles. Professional, friendly, and pleasant, it was little wonder Randy Wayne Davis was the first face staff, volunteers, and visitors encountered at PCI.

"Morning, Chaplain," he said through the slot next to the document tray. "How are you?"

Both the slot and tray were built in to the control room. Made of heavy metal, they represented the only access points to the control room from the exterior of the prison. They were used for everything from law enforcement checking their weapons before entering the institution, to staff, volunteers, and visitors signing in and out, and passing paperwork.

"Good," I said, leaning down a little to make sure he could hear me. "You?"

"All good in the hood," he said. "Hard not to be

happy on a day like this."

I turned and considered the day. He was right. It was a brilliant, beautiful morning.

"Is Ms. Rodden coming in today?"

"She might be in later," I said. "She's not feeling well at the moment."

He nodded as if he knew why and sympathized. "Hope it's just a little morning sickness and nothing more."

"It is. Thanks."

"I've got a few messages for her," he said. "Should I just . . ."

"I'll take them," I said. "Make sure she gets them."

He dropped several pink phone message slips into the drawer and slid it toward me. "Some in there for you too."

"Thanks."

I took the slips but didn't look through them.

"You okay, Chaplain?" Randy Wayne asked.

I nodded.

"Sure? You seem a little . . . I don't know, distracted."

"Sorry," I said. "Didn't realize. Just thinking about what I have to do today."

"No need to apologize. Just makin' sure. Figure somebody should check on *you* occasionally."

"Thanks. I'm good."

"Well, have a good day," he said.

"You too."

I moved back over to the gate, held up my ID, and he buzzed me in. I had to wait a little longer than normal inside the sally port, because of a phone call that came into the control room, but eventually he buzzed me through the second gate and onto the compound.

Chapter Seven

"CHAPLAIN. CHAPLAIN."

I was walking toward the chapel trying to appear as normal as possible, while wondering where and how Anna was, when I heard Sergeant Helm's rough voice yelling for me.

When I turned, I saw that she was motioning me over to the mailroom window on the back of the visiting park.

"I just heard," she said.

It was a very small town and news traveled fast—particularly bad news—but it surprised me that word of Chris Taunton's death was already making the rounds.

"What's that?" I asked.

"About Richie," she said.

Oh. That.

"And after what happened to Hahn . . ."

So much death. I'm surrounded by it. Death beside me. Death before me. Death behind me. Death on all sides.

"Are you okay?"

Carrie Helms was fifty-eight years old and looked it. Not in a bad way. She just looked her age. She wore too much makeup, and she misapplied it—an action that emphasized her wrinkles, but she had a vibrancy about her, a youthful gleam in the big blue eyes that twinkled beneath her short gray hair.

I nodded.

"You sure? You seem . . . distracted."

"I'm just tired. Maybe a little drained."

"Why wouldn't you be? You singlehandedly stopped those—"

"I didn't singlehandedly do anything. Merrill. Anna. My dad. Even Jake. Lots of people worked together to—"

"Everybody's talkin' about it," she said. "How did you figure out what was going on in Medical?"

"I really need to get to the chapel. Can we talk about it a little later?"

"Oh, sure. Drop by later when you can. Is Anna coming in today?"

"She's pretty sick," I said. "Probably not."

"Then bring your lunch down here and eat with me, and we can talk then."

Chapter Eight

I was in my office, the desultory sounds of Gregorian chant drifting around the room, counseling an inmate named Kevin whose grandmother, the woman who raised him, had recently died, when Bat Matson, the warden, walked in without knocking.

When I first started at PCI, Edward Stone, a fastidious, aging African-American man, had been the warden. He had presented certain challenges for me, and I for him, but eventually we had settled into a relatively comfortable working relationship—something that had not happened with Bat Matson, and wasn't likely to.

A fleshy man in his early sixties with prominent jowls and thick gray hair swooped to the side, Matson, a man as harsh and rigid in his work as his fundamentalist religion, was wearing what I had come to think of as his uniform—cheap black tie, white cotton shirt with button-down collar, black poly/cotton flat-front work pants, and black Polyurethane lace-up shoes. Never a coat. Never any color. Never any style or creativity. Never any variation or alteration.

He was accompanied by an athletic youngish woman with shoulder-length blondish-brown hair, cinnamon-tinged skin, and stunning grayish-green eyes.

"Inmate," Matson said, "wait outside in the hallway until we're done."

Without hesitation, Kevin jumped up and headed toward the door, nodding deferentially toward Matson and the woman as he did.

"Wait," I said, standing. "Kevin just lost his grandmother. We're in the middle of a very—"

"It's okay," Kevin said. "I'm fine. I'll be out here when you're done, Chaplain."

With that, he exited the room as quickly as possible, closing the door behind him.

"Most of what I do here is crisis counseling," I said to Matson. "You can't keep barging in when I'm in the middle of it."

"My institution," he said. "I can go anywhere in it anytime I like. Don't like it, you can resign."

"I appreciate you being reasonable about it," I said.

The beautiful young woman with him smiled.

Matson sat down in one of the seats across from my desk. The young woman in the one beside him. After she did, I sat back down in mine.

"This is Rachel Peterson," he said, tossing a thumb in her direction. "She's the new IG of the department. She's investigating the death of the psych specialist and the arrests of the medical personnel and your involvement. Give her your full cooperation."

I smiled and nodded at her. "Nice to meet you."

The previous Inspector General of the Department of Corrections had been my ex-father-in-law, Tom Daniels. I had worked with him some. Like my marriage to his daughter, it had not ended well. I hadn't spoken with either of them for quite a while, though recently I had been trying unsuccessfully to get in touch with Susan. Maybe it was time to try Tom.

Merrill and even Anna asked why I felt the need to attempt to reconnect with Susan or Tom or Sarah, why I couldn't just let it lie where it died. I had never been able to answer them to either their or my satisfaction. It was just something I felt I had to do, an intuition common and familiar to me—the ones I so often let guide me through my life. In addition to whatever else it was, part of my motivation was part of what made me who I am. I wanted peace if possible. Connection. An open channel of communication so that I might minister or help in some way one day.

"Nice to meet you," Rachel said, extending her hand across the desk to shake mine.

There was something in her voice—plenty of Southern drawl, but something else besides, something just under the drawl.

"Where'd you grow up?" I asked.

"All over. Military brat."

I nodded.

Her hands were strong, her shake firm without being aggressively so.

And it wasn't just her hands. Her entire build and bearing were strong and solid—something her mind and spirit had to mirror for her to be the first woman to hold the position she did.

Anna would like her. She would like Anna. Have to make sure they meet.

"I'm gonna leave you two to it," Matson said, sliding to the edge of his chair but not standing. "But before I do . . . I heard what happened last night . . . about your involvement with the conclusion of the Potter Farm incident. Seems there might not have been a conclusion if it weren't for you."

It was the closest thing to a compliment he had ever given me.

"I think you're a better investigator than I realized," he said. "I mean it. I'm saying this because if you're cleared by Miss Peterson for what happened here, I want you two to talk about you becoming our institutional inspector."

Without another word, he stood and left, the door banging loudly behind him as he did.

"I understand my predecessor was your father-in-law."

I nodded.

"And that you're the reason he's my predecessor instead of still in this position."

I shrugged.

"Are you interested in being the institutional inspector here?"

I shook my head.

"Anywhere?"

I shook my head again.

"You gonna cooperate with my investigation?"

I nodded.

"Are you going to attempt to do so without uttering a single word?"

I smiled. "No," I said. "I'll be downright chatty if you like."

"Because you did nothing wrong? Have nothing to hide?"

"That's for you to say."

"What do you say?"

"I did plenty wrong," I said, "but not in the sense you mean. Nothing illegal. Just meant mistakes. And I have nothing to hide."

"Everybody has something to hide," she said.

"Even the first female Inspector General of the

Florida Department of Corrections?"

She smiled.

She had a dark complexion and bright white teeth, and her eyes and teeth shined brilliantly when she smiled.

"Even her."

We were quiet a moment.

"I'm happy to answer all your questions," I said, "but do you mind if I finish with Kevin first?"

"Not at all," she said. "I'll come back right after lunch. How's that?"

"Thank you."

"All my questions really come down to the same thing," she said. "You can be thinking about it until we meet."

"Okay."

"Did your actions lead to the death of your coworker? Are you responsible for Hahn Ling's death?"

Chapter Nine

After I finished with Kevin, I got an outside line from the control room and punched in the old number I had for Tom Daniels.

To my surprise he answered.

"You son of a bitch," he said. "You know, don't you? I knew it. I told them you—"

"Know what?"

"What'd you call for?" he asked, the tone of his voice changing.

I wondered what he meant, but knew with someone like him it could be anything.

Of all the cases I had worked over the years, only a handful still haunted me. Chief among them was the Atlanta Child Murders, but way up on the list was the case that involved Tom Daniels.

Not solving a case was one kind of agony, but solving it and being unable to bring about any kind of justice was a special kind of torture. Daniels was the latter, and that he could be a free man, free to inflict more harm, commit more crime, was particularly difficult for me to take—something that required much prayer, meditation, and letting go. And I had been doing okay with it, but hearing his voice, having him say he knew I would figure out something else—something no doubt duplicitous—he was up to, brought it all back, and made me feel the familiar old frustration that had too often eaten away at my insides over the years.

"What are you doing, Tom?" I asked.

"None of your business, *John*."

"I called to see how you were doing," I said. "To check on Susan. She's not . . . She went from not answering to changing her number."

"She wants nothing to do with you. None of us do. Don't call. Don't write. Don't come by. Don't even think about us. Haven't you hurt us enough? Leave us the fuck alone."

That was so typical of the criminal mentality. He was the one who had done all the damage, the one who had hurt so many people, yet he was blaming someone else for it. A victim until the end, his wounded, paranoid, defensive paradigm would always justify, always blame, and never take responsibility for any of his actions, not even murder.

"*Hurt you enough?*" I said.

"You're toxic John. Far sicker than even you realize. I'm so glad my little girl got away from you. Probably the only reason she's alive today."

"I met your successor today," I said.

"You know how many guys she had to fuck to get that job?" he said. "They call her Rug Burn Rachel. Have you fucked her yet? Y'all are perfect for each other. I'm sure she'll do just fine for you if you don't get—"

He stopped abruptly.

"If I don't get what?"

"Good talk, John. Go fuck yourself. And don't call back. Susan had the right idea. I'm changing my number too."

With that, he hung up, leaving me to sit there with

the receiver in my hand, seething.

"Grant me the serenity to accept the things I can't change, the courage to change the things I can, and the wisdom to know the difference," I said.

I was in the chapel alone.

Lights off, votive candles lit, music playing softly.

Trying to let go.

Stop clinging. End your attachment to the outcome. Let go.

I centered myself, or attempted to, by concentrating on my breathing and repeating the Serenity Prayer over and over.

"Accept the things I can't change."

Accept. Release. Embrace. Let go.

"Courage to change the things I can."

Yourself. Your thinking. You are all you can change. Let go of all of this, of everything. Anna is all that matters.

Reminding myself of that helped more than anything else.

"Does that work?" Rachel asked.

She had walked into the chapel and up the side aisle and was standing a few feet away.

"If you work it," I said without thinking about it.

"That's an AA thing, isn't it?"

"It is," I said, "but it applies."

"And how's all that working for you?"

"See previous answer," I said. "Works well when I work it. It's all a practice. We get good at what we practice."

She nodded thoughtfully.

I glanced at the clock on the back wall as I stood up.

I had intended to go up and have lunch with Carrie Helms, but without realizing it I had spent my entire lunch hour plus a few minutes of the state's time in here.

"Sorry to interrupt," she said. "I knocked and called out in the hallway."

"No problem," I said. "Lost track of time."

"With your practice."

I couldn't tell if she was mocking me, but decided if she was, it was only mildly.

"Yes."

"Is part of what you're processing Hahn Ling's death?"

I sat down on the front pew and she joined me.

"Sure."

"What else?"

"A delightful conversation I had with your predecessor not too long after you left last time."

She smiled and nodded. "If anything could give you religion . . . What'd he say about me?"

"Nothin'."

"You're not supposed to lie."

"Why?"

"It's like a chaplain rule or something. Tell me. I'm a big girl. I can take it."

"I can't remember."

"Come on. Tell me."

"He may have insinuated that you got your job by means other than merit."

She smiled. "*May have insinuated.* You're a gentleman, John Jordan. I'll give you that. Let me guess . . . Rug Burn Rachel. I get that one a lot."

I neither confirmed nor denied.

"Bet it gives his misogynist ass a special kind of heartburn that a woman has his old job," she said.

"It's called a nontaxable bonus," I said.

She laughed out loud at that.

"I'm gonna be straight with you," she said. "If I were you, I'd get a lawyer. The outcome of the investigation doesn't just determine departmental disciplinary actions, but could result in criminal charges as well."

Chapter Ten

End of the work day, and all I could think about was getting home and waiting for the call to come.

Exhausted. Sleepy. Tired of this nod toward normalcy. Ready to find out what I had to do to get Anna back and start doing it.

I was locking the chapel when Merrill walked up.

As usual, his pristine correctional officer uniform curved the contours of his muscles as if it had been tailored to do so, his dark brown skin, roughly the hue of his pants, contrasting nicely with the lighter brown of his shirt.

I hadn't seen him today. In truth, I had been avoiding him. If anyone could sense something was wrong, it was this perceptive and insightful man who had been my closest companion and confidant since childhood.

"'Sup, Chap?" he said, his voice rich with playfulness.

I pretended to be having trouble with the key to give myself a moment to prepare. As I did, he stood easily, waited patiently, nodding to the end-of-shift staff and officers passing by. His companionship was comfortable in the way only a lifelong friend could be—something that made it even more difficult not to unburden onto him, not to bring him into the confidence he had proven himself worthy of before we were ever out of junior high school. And an infinite number of times since.

"New IG interview you?" he asked.

"Started to, then told me to get a lawyer and she'd be back tomorrow."

"What I heard, they's one less lawyer in the world today," he said.

He was referring to Chris Taunton. Word of his death was out. Dad had taken care of it.

"It ain't the ninety-nine on the bottom of the ocean floor, but it still a good start. Hella good start, you ask me."

"He's probably not who I would've hired anyway," I said.

"Shoulda let a brotha know you's gonna take him out. Woulda liked to be in on that. Least let me help you hide the body."

I turned from the door to face him for the first time.

"Didn't want to risk you gettin' hit with an accessory-after-the-fact rap."

"My nigga. Always thinkin' of others, ain't you?"

We started walking toward the front gate and the daily parole that awaited us there. The compound around us was littered with our coworkers doing the same thing.

"Anna okay?" he asked.

I nodded. "Morning sickness."

"Even this late in the PM?"

"Hope not. Find out in a few."

"Be nice not havin' to deal with Chris in raisin' the kid," he said.

"Yes it will."

We walked a little ways in silence.

The late afternoon sun suffused everything with a soft golden glow, making even the prison sparkle and shimmer.

"You ain't gonna ask what the IG asked me?" he said.

"Figured you'd tell me anything you thought I needed to know."

"Offered me immunity to testify against you."

I shook my head.

"Asked her what you had to do with the tactical team shooting first and finding out what was goin' on later. Probably still don't know. She said you were the reason it got to that point. When I ask how the hell she can think that, she said it based on the other testimonies she has. Who you think tellin' tales?"

I shrugged. "No tellin'. Take your pick."

We reached the sally port and were buzzed into it. Holding our IDs up to the control room window, we were then buzzed through the other gate and into the world again.

"Don't seem too worried about it," he said.

"Practicing letting go and living the Serenity Prayer."

"Oh, 'cause it look like you just don't give a fuck. What's goin' on?"

"Just tired. Didn't sleep."

"You never sleep."

"Upset about Hahn. Utterly and completely spent."

He nodded and we continued walking through the employee parking lot toward our vehicles.

We reached Anna's Mustang first. I popped the locks and set my briefcase in the passenger seat.

"Nice ride," he said. "If it were anybody but Anna I'd ask if you were with her for the car."

I attempted a smile.

"You don't remember when I was born, do you?" he asked.

I shook my head. "I was busy tryin' to be born myself."

"Well, it was night," he said. "Just not *last* night. You don't have to tell me what's goin' on, but don't kid yourself that I buy there's not anything. Chris dead. Anna not here. You so deep inside yourself it like you not there."

Chapter Eleven

Waiting. Again.

Alone.

Dark trailer. Quiet night. Sounds of breathing.

Occasionally, I'd catch myself dozing and shake myself awake.

Eventually, the call came.

"Are you ready?" he asked.

"I am."

"You did good today," he said. "Could've done better. But it appeared you pulled off a seemingly ordinary day."

Did he know about my visit with Chris? Did he know he was alive?

"I have a few eyes around," he said. "I'm not going to lie to you and tell you I see your every move or anything like that. I'm counting on your love for your lady to make you do the right thing, but I'm keeping tabs on you too."

"Then you know I haven't said or done anything other than what you instructed me to do."

"It appears that way."

"How is Anna?"

"She is fine. She'll tell you herself in a minute."

I didn't say anything and we were quiet a moment.

"You said you'd do anything to get the girl back," he said.

"Just tell me what."

"There's a young man in your institution," he said. "His mother is dying. Doesn't have much time left. She wants to see her son before she . . . His requests for furloughs have been denied. His hardship petition rejected. Higher-ups in the state are friends of the family. They can do nothing. Every available option has been exhausted. The family has hired me to get their son out of your prison, and I'm *hiring* you."

"To break an inmate out of a maximum security prison?"

"Uh huh."

"Something many claim is impossible these days."

"Is it?" he asked. "What do you say?"

"It *is* extremely difficult," I said. "Nearly impossible."

"Nearly? Can you do it? For the girl?"

"Yes."

"I will trade her for him."

"What's his name?" I asked. "When do you want to make the trade and where?"

"How long will you need?"

"Depends on who he is," I said. "His custody level, job assignment. But obviously I'd like to do it as soon as possible."

"And you're sure you can."

"What I'm sure of is that I can figure it out."

"Without involving anyone else? On your own."

"Yes."

"We will make the exchange two nights from now, the night of the blood moon. That gives you tomorrow to prepare."

"How about tomorrow night?"

"Too soon. I want you coming up with a great plan that leaves nothing to chance. You'll need tomorrow to make preparations. Your wife is safe and well taken care of. I assure you. Here. I'll let her assure you."

There was a pause, then some rustling, then her.

"John?"

"Are you okay?"

"I really am," she said. "Bored. Ready to see you. But they're being really good to me."

"I love you. I'm gonna get you back."

"I know. I love you. Miss you so much. Need you. Need you to hold me."

"How's the baby? How're you feeling?"

"Everything is good. Seriously. It's a little crazy how well they're taking care of me. Keeping me comfortable and hydrated and fed and catering to my every need—well every one but you."

"What's my favorite food?" I asked.

"Pizza."

"Let's get some when we're back together."

"New York pizza with extra cheese. And garlic knots."

"Anything you want," I said.

The next voice was not hers.

"Satisfied?" he said. "I am taking better care of her than you do."

"Not possible, but keep trying."

"I'll call you tomorrow with the details," he said.

"I can't figure out how to do it without knowing who it is."

"Oh, I don't believe that at all," he said, and ended the call.

Chapter Twelve

She got off the phone with John feeling reassured and hopeful.

He had that effect on her.

God, I miss him. Please let me see him again soon. Don't let the short time we had together be all we get. Please.

She thought about what she should do.

She was blindfolded and had yet to see anything. Should she keep it that way or try to work it off a little, sneak a peek at her captors and this place of captivity.

What would John do?

She smiled. WWJJD. What Would John Jordan Do? If she survived this ordeal, she would have bracelets made.

What would he do or what would he have me do? They're not necessarily the same thing.

He'd want me to seize any opportunity I was given, but not try to make any, not yet. He'd want me to do what they say, protect myself. Not worry about getting myself out. Let him do it.

Listen.

Someone walked back into the room.

That's what you can do. Listen carefully. Hear everything. Make mental notes on every ambient sound, on every word uttered and how they are uttered. Use your hearing to take in everything. Be able to give a full description based on what you hear.

I can do that.

Start now.

Where am I?

A cabin?

Why cabin? Why not farm house or just house?

Feels rustic and isolated.

It does, doesn't it? That's good. What else?

There's water nearby. I can feel it more than hear it. Some added moisture in the air. A lake? Maybe, but—no, it's moving. A river. I'm in a cabin by the river.

I'm on a bed. An uncomfortable bed. Propped up on pillows. Wrists bound and tied to—what? A headboard? A bedpost?

She moved her hands around, her fingers feeling about.

"Is it too tight?" the younger of the two men asked.

Actually, it wasn't. The restraints were padded and loose—long enough so that she could move her arms around some, but not long enough so that she could reach her blindfold and rip it off.

"Hand was just falling asleep. It's fine."

How closely must they be watching me?

The headboard was flat so she wasn't sure what her restraints were tied to, but it was definitely a headboard.

"Sorry you have to be restrained at all," he said. "I just don't want to take a chance on anything going wrong, don't want anything to happen to prevent this all from going as smoothly as possible. Don't want you even accidentally seeing me or . . . anyone."

She nodded.

"No mess-ups. No one getting hurt. Everybody getting what they want. You want to go home, right? I want that too. For both of us. I'm just trying to ensure that's what will happen."

She nodded and actually thanked him.

What was that? You're not suffering from Stockholm already, are you?

Of course not. But why did I thank him? I guess I—well, they're being so good to me, and I guess I believe him, think he really does mean what he said.

What does he sound like? Listen to his speech patterns, accent, vocabulary. Figure him out by what he says—and what he doesn't say.

Young. The one who does most of the talking—and all the talking to John—sounds like a kid. Not a child, but a young man in late adolescence or in his early twenties.

There's a quality to his voice, a resonance. Even for as young as he sounds, he speaks with authority, his voice eliciting trust.

It's also . . . what . . . professional. As if he could be a radio talk show host or a guy who does voice-over work. Something like that.

Commit his voice to memory. Don't forget what he sounds like.

I never will. Even when I'll want to, I won't be able to.

The other guy rarely speaks. He's older. How much, I can't be sure. But I'm pretty sure he is. His voice doesn't have nearly the richness and resonance of the talker. That's what I'll call the younger one—Talker.

What to call the other one. There's something about the way he smells. What is it?

And then something occurs to her.

Is there a third? One who has never spoken a single word? One who smells different from the one who doesn't speak much at all.

There is.

At least I think there is. I guess the one could smell different at different times, but . . .

She'd have to pay closer attention—not just focus on how they sound, but on how they smell.

But then she thought . . .

None of it matters anyway. They'll never let me go.

Chapter Thirteen

Escaping from prison is next to impossible.

Perhaps there was a time when an inmate who really set his mind to it could figure a way out, but those days are long gone.

Today the prison system is high tech and high security with an emphasis on careful custody of inmates. Experts and engineers have designed modern prisons for ultimate control over the inmate population, dictating their every move, ensuring escapes are a thing of the past, which they mostly were.

One of the last notable escapes from within a Florida state prison happened when a group of inmates spent weeks tunneling out of the chapel beneath the baptistry and came out on the other side of the perimeter fence. The crime writer Elmore Leonard even used it in one of his books, which later became a movie with George Clooney and Jennifer Lopez. Since then, an inordinate amount of additional security measures had been put in place—including a second perimeter fence even farther out with coils and coils of razor wire. And now there were no buildings within a hundred yards of the outside fences.

About the only escapes that occurred these days were by inmates already outside the institution—inmates who worked on an outside grounds crew, those on furlough or being transported to court or to a hospital for a medical procedure—but even these were extremely rare because of all the procedures and protections in place.

If the inmate I was trading for Anna worked outside the institution, and the chances of that were extremely slim, getting him away from the correctional officers guarding him would still be unimaginably daunting, but if I had to break him out from inside, the task would become infinitely more difficult.

If he's inside the prison and has to be broken out, what are my options?

There aren't many.

Fake an illness and try to get him on an ambulance—something problematic on too many levels to count.

Create a diversion or distraction of some kind and . . . Even if I could, that wouldn't help me get him through the several locked doors and gates and past the control room sergeant who has to identify him before he buzzes the gate open.

What if I had him switch places with another inmate working outside the fence? He'd have to be his twin—resemble enough to fool the correctional officer in the dorm, at the gate, and on the work crew—and the other inmate would have to be willing to switch places with him, something that wouldn't benefit him in any way and would add a lot of time to his sentence.

I could try the same thing with a staff member. Finding one who resembled him even a little would be nearly impossible. Finding one who would agree to do it, and risk losing his job and going to jail, would be impossible.

And even if I could figure a way to do any of the above, I'd still have to be able to make it past the control room sergeant looking at faces and comparing them to IDs—something he or she does every single day, someone who knows the staff intimately.

So far every scenario I had considered involved some form of deception in an attempt to sneak the inmate out of the institution. It showed just how desperate I was that I even considered the possibility of a literal breakout next.

Breaking into a prison and then breaking an inmate out is as incredible a proposition as the ridiculous and farfetched movies made about such things.

First, you'd need a vehicle that could even attempt it—one especially designed to do it. An actual military tank or armored law enforcement riot control vehicle came to mind as the only vehicles that might even stand a chance.

Even if you could find a vehicle that could break through the main gate, with its cement pilings and steel cable reinforcements, that would only get you into the sally port, and in a prime spot to be ambushed by the armed officer in Tower I and the armed response team on the ground while facing the second gate. And even if you could somehow get through the second gate, that would only get you on the upper compound with the chapel, Medical, Education, Food Services, etc., and if by some miracle you made it through there, you'd again face two more gates and Tower II. You'd then have to be able to break into the locked dorm where the inmate was located and then possibly another locked door and a cell door, depending on his custody level. Then you'd have to return through a gauntlet of prison response teams, local law enforcement, and possibly the National Guard, depending on their response time.

Of course, you could come through a perimeter fence—well, the two razor wire–covered perimeter fences, which would immediately trigger an alarm in the control room, then continue through a series of other fences while being fired at by the towers and response teams, your vehicle covered by the looping razor wire designed to collapse in on whatever goes through it.

If breaking into the prison with a vehicle especially built to do such things wasn't impossible, it was the next thing to it.

The other breakout scenario that came to mind was landing a helicopter on the rec yard or in the field between the chapel and the perimeter fence. You'd have to have a chopper, a pilot willing to do it, which meant involving others in the plan, you'd have to do it while being fired at, and you'd have to coordinate the landing with the inmate's movements and hope somehow he wouldn't be shot as he ran toward and climbed aboard the chopper.

Again, not entirely impossible. Just nearly entirely impossible.

I abandoned thoughts about the *how* for a few moments to think about the *who*.

Who could the inmate be?

Not many inmates in the state prison system come from families with money.

Had I counseled any inmates lately whose mothers were sick?

Of course, the caller could be lying about the motive—probably was. It could be a simple lie—a different loved one sick or a completely different but still benevolent motive, or it could be an altogether dark motive and the inmate's life could be in danger.

If the last, would it change anything? Would I not only risk losing my job and doing jail time, but actually deliver an inmate to be tortured or killed to save Anna?

I would. *I will. I have to.*

If I can keep the inmate from escaping, regardless of the motive, I will, but getting Anna back is far and away the first priority.

The kidnapper was putting me into a position of seeing what I was capable of on a lot of different levels. Under nearly all other circumstances, I'd never consider aiding the escape of an inmate—no matter the reason. But . . .

Anna trumps all.

He'd mentioned that Thursday night, the night we were supposed to trade Anna for the inmate, was a blood moon. Though I had heard the term, I wasn't sure exactly what that was, so I took a minute and looked it up.

A blood moon is a total lunar eclipse of a full moon.

The earth casts its shadow on the moon. The sun's rays that still manage to reach the moon travel through the earth's atmosphere, turning the light dark red.

Some see a blood moon as an omen or portent, a sign in the sky of great spiritual significance.

The sun will turn into darkness, and the moon into blood, before the great and terrible day of the Lord.

Chapter Fourteen

That night I dreamed of Suicide Kings, Wayne Williams, Hahn Ling, Martin Fisher, and my mom's funeral.

Graveside. At Mom's funeral. The living and the dead side by side in the folding chairs on the green AstroTurf spread out beneath the small awning and before the dark wooden casket.

Mom was among them. Smiling at me, nodding her support of what I was saying to comfort those mourning her passing.

I'm so proud of you, she mouthed.

Danny Jacobs was sitting beside his mom, Cheryl. You couldn't tell one was dead and one was alive.

Dad's old Irish Setter, Wallace, was sitting just outside the tent on the grass, tongue out, panting loudly, his red hair shining in the sun.

Wallace had been dead a while. Dad's inseparable companion for much of his too-short life, he had gotten sick and not left Dad's house during the last several years before he died.

Why hadn't Dad replaced him? Grief? Busyness? Had he found companionship somewhere else? Why hadn't I asked him?

Martin Fisher was next to LaMarcus Williams.

Where is Anna? Why isn't she here?

"The faceless man has her," Martin Fisher said aloud, though I hadn't voiced my thoughts.

"You've got to get her back," LaMarcus said. "And fast."

"She's not here so she's not dead," I said.

"That's not necessarily true, my brother," Wayne Williams said. "People can be dead and you not even know it."

The two Mollys were sitting together on the second row of chairs.

Molly Gellar was a nurse I had dated briefly when I first moved back to Pottersville from Atlanta. Molly Thomas was the wife on an inmate involved in the first investigation I had conducted at PCI.

"She's not dead," Molly Thomas said, her hair still wet and matted from where she had been pulled from the river.

"She can't be," Molly Gellar added, bullet hole still in her head, the small round wound haloed by a reddish abrasion ring and the darker tattooing, stippling, and burn marks of the barrel.

"People can be dead and *they* not even know it," Williams added.

"Don't listen to them, honey," Mom said. "We're all alive—and all dead, I guess. Go back to the eulogy."

Suddenly there was an inmate in the last chair on the last row.

No matter how hard I looked, I couldn't really see him.

"I've got a question," I said. "How can I break him out of PCI?"

"You can't," Hahn said. "We all die there."

"You'll lose your job," Molly Gellar said.

"You'd go to jail," Molly Thomas said.

"It's easy," the inmate said. "I have to be someone else."

I nodded.

"Can't be me," he added.

"But how? How can you be somebody else?"

"Put that big brain of yours to work on it," Jordan Moore said.

She hadn't been there before. Now she was sitting in the front row looking as fresh as the morning and beautiful as ever.

She was my first college girlfriend. She had been so much more than a girlfriend. She was the embodiment of pain and tragedy for me like few people were.

"You'll figure it out."

I woke haunted.

Not afraid or disturbed, just haunted.

I missed my mom. Was she really dead?

I missed many of the others who attended her funeral in my dream, and felt as if I had just spent actual time with them. Now they were all gone. I was alone and lonely.

If I could just roll over and touch Anna, hold her and have her whisper how much she loves me.

But she too was gone.

And in her absence I was utterly alone.

Chapter Fifteen

The call that came the next morning wasn't the one I was waiting for.

"Chris Taunton is asking to see you again," Dad said. "Says it's extremely urgent and important. What's going on?"

"With him? I have no idea."

"Why's he talkin' to you and not us?"

"I was surprised when he asked to see me the first time," I said. "I'm even more surprised this time."

"You know more than you're saying," he said.

I had nothing for that so I left it alone.

"You gonna go see him?" he asked.

"Not sure," I said. "Don't want to. But I'm curious about what he has to say."

"Would you go for me?" Dad said. "Let me know what he has to say."

"Okay."

"How are you?" he asked. "I mean about your mom and everything."

Still haunted by the dream, I was unable to answer.

I waited for a while but no call came.

I spent some time in prayer and meditation, showered and dressed. Still no call.

Drove to the hospital with my phone in my hand, held it the entire time I talked to Chris Taunton, but the call never came.

"Have they made contact yet?" Chris asked. "What do they want?"

"How're you feeling?"

"Like shit. What did they say? Is she okay?"

"Seems so. I think she is."

"What do they want? Do they know I'm still alive?"

"Don't think they do."

"We could use that."

I shook my head.

"Let me help."

"Do what?" I asked. "You can't even sit up. And I'm not going to do anything but what they say."

"What did they say? What do they want?"

"Get better, Chris."

"You're playing with Anna's life. Let me—"

"I'm not playing at all."

"Why won't you let me help?"

"Already told you."

"You've got an unknown—something they know nothing about. Use it. We can go back to hating each other after she's back safe and okay."

"I don't hate you, Chris."

"Then I'll go back to hating you. But until then, let's do all we can to make sure she gets back safely so I have something to hate you for."

I shook my head again. "I've got to go."

"What if you fail?" he said. "Somebody should know what's going on, what you were trying to do."

I nodded. "You're right. Somebody will."

As I drove to work, phone in hand, I thought about what Chris had said.

I couldn't use him, could I?

He was in no shape. I didn't trust him. I didn't want to do anything but what they said to do.

Is that the wrong play? Am I making a mistake? Not using the one element of surprise I have?

He was right about one thing. I needed a contingency plan in case something went wrong. But what?

When I pulled up to the prison and saw Merrill in the parking lot I knew what.

I parked beside him and got out, pausing a minute to look at my phone one last time.

Why hadn't I heard from the kidnapper this morning? What should I do?

Cell phones weren't allowed inside the institution. The caller seemed to know a lot, but maybe he didn't know that.

What if he calls while I'm inside?

I could try to sneak the phone in—something risky and very difficult to do—or I could come out here and check it often.

All staff entering the institution each morning were subjected to a full search. Depending on which officers conducted them, the searches were far more thorough sometimes than others. I could hide it somewhere and act as if I had forgotten it, but chances were it'd be found.

Of course, I could just not go into the institution, but the kidnapper had emphasized again for me to have the most normal day possible.

"Anna still sick?"

I nodded, dropped the phone on the seat, and locked her car. "Gettin' better though."

Across the lot, I saw Rachel Peterson pull up and park next to the warden in front of Admin.

"Need a favor," I said. "It's important."

"Name it."

"It's the no-questions-asked kind."

He nodded. "Lot of yours are."

Are they? I'd never thought about it, but I guess they were. And yet he always responded the same way. Name it. You got it. Shore thang boss. Shoot.

"Tomorrow night. If I don't call you by one, there'll be a note in my trailer explaining why and what to do about it."

"K."

"Thanks. Thank you."

"You said no questions asked, but . . . This not somethin' I can be involved in before one?"

"Wish to God it were," I said.

Rachel Peterson had been lingering by her car, evidently waiting for us to reach her.

"Workin' on your story?" she asked.

"We're caught in a trap," Merrill said.

Her eyes widened.

I smiled.

"Can't walk out," I said.

"Why can't you see what you're doin' to me?" Merrill asked.

I could see it dawn on her, followed by what was almost a smile twitching in her lips. "Cute," she said. "But my mind is only suspicious of suspicious people."

"Of course it is," Merrill said in his most condescending you're-full-of-shit voice.

Chapter Sixteen

"**W**ere you told to stay out of the investigation into the apparent suicides here at the institution?" Rachel Peterson asked.

"I was."

"By who?"

Whom popped into my head but not out of my mouth. I wasn't in the habit of correcting anyone's grammar, and no matter how hostile this interview might become, I had no plans to resort to anything like that.

"The warden and the interim institutional investigator," I said.

We were in my office at my insistence, an accommodation she seemed willing enough to make.

I wanted to be here in case the kidnapper called my office phone, but she probably thought it was so I could feel more comfortable and secure. That she was willing to conduct the interview here demonstrated her confidence in my guilt and in her ability to break me. I had told her it was because I was the only chaplain on duty and needed to be in the chapel to supervise the inmates and be available for emergencies.

She was sitting across the desk from me in one of the two chairs normally occupied by inmates, a small digital recorder between us, its red indicator light on. She wore dark well-fitting jeans, a white button-down, and round-toed Justin Gypsy Roper boots. Her longish brown hair was gathered into a ponytail, and she looked more like a modern cowgirl than the IG of the Florida DOC.

"Did you?" she asked.

"Did I what?" I asked.

"Did you still investigate?"

"Some, maybe, but not really," I said. "I didn't have access to the investigation so I was on the outside. Wasn't much I could do."

"But you still did some investigating on your own?" she said.

"A little, yes, but—"

"Even after you were told not to?"

"Yes."

"What were you about to say?" she asked.

"Huh?"

"You said *but* like you were about to say something else."

"Oh."

"You seem distracted. Are you okay?"

She held nothing, never looked at a note, never wrote anything down, just kept her brilliant blue-green-gray eyes intently trained on me.

"I was going to say that at a certain point in the investigation the interim inspector asked for my help and began to involve me more."

"He did?"

I nodded.

"Verbal responses for the recording, please," she said.

"Yes," I said. "He did."

"It's your testimony that the institutional inspector asked the chaplain to help with his investigation?"

"He asked me. I'm the chaplain. So yes."

"Why would he do that?" she asked. "Why would he and the warden tell you to stay out of the investigation and then ask you to join in? Why would a trained investigator ask a chaplain to assist in a possible homicide investigation?"

"Because of my background. I was an investigator before I became a chaplain. As to why he changed his mind and asked for my help after telling me he didn't want it, you'd have to ask him. He told me it was because he needed help with the investigation, that he really wanted the job of institutional inspector and he thought clearing his first case would help him get it."

"But he didn't clear it. You did."

I shrugged. "It was a group effort. His case. His clear."

"I've interviewed Inspector Lawson," she said. "He and the warden both say they told you to stay out of the investigation, but he never mentioned asking you later to join it."

"Regardless," I said, "it's what happened."

"According to you."

"Yes," I said. "According to me."

"Okay, we'll come back to that. What were you doing in the dorm when Hahn Ling was killed?"

"Trying to save her."

"How'd you know she needed saving? Why didn't you report it to the inspector?"

"When I regained consciousness, I—"

"You had been drugged, is that right?"

I nodded.

"Verbal," she said.

"Yes. When I regained consciousness I was told where she was and with whom. I was also told that she had mentioned something in front of the killer that would let him know we were closing in on him. The inspector had made two arrests and was up in Admin waiting for FDLE. We were in Medical."

"We?"

"Sergeant Monroe and myself. We rushed down to the dorm to try to save her."

"You had been unconscious?"

"Yes."

"So you were still woozy, not thinking clearly."

"I was thinking just fine."

"According to you. But you would think that, wouldn't you? You acted in a manner you shouldn't have even if you had had all your wits, but you were severely compromised because of the drugs you had been administered. Shouldn't you have reported what you knew instead of rushing down to the dorm while you were still dazed and not able to think? Would Ms. Ling be alive if you had?"

Rachel Peterson was a professional. She never raised her voice, never took too strong a tone, mostly remained flat, with only the occasional hint of disbelief and eyebrow raised incredulously.

"I wasn't dazed or unable to think. We had the situation under control, had talked the inmate into surrendering, into letting Hahn go, and then he was killed by the response team sniper and—"

"Who gave the order to fire?"

"I have no idea. Never heard one given. The shot was fired before the response team rushed into the quad. If they hadn't come in, if the sniper hadn't fired the shot, Hahn would still be alive. And we wouldn't be having this conversation."

"You keep referring to Ms. Ling as Hahn. You were intimate with her. Is that correct?"

"No, it's not. She was a coworker, a friend. Someone I referred to by her first name—like most of the people I know."

"But you had an intimate relationship with her. You dated her."

"We weren't intimate. We went on a few casual dates some six months or more before any of this happened."

"You're not a very typical chaplain, are you?"

"What do you mean?"

"Doesn't matter. Not relevant."

Before I could press her to say more, my phone rang and I lunged for it.

"Chaplain Jordan."

It was the warden's secretary saying Rachel Peterson was needed in Admin.

"Tell her I'll be up in a few," she said.

I did.

"So—" Rachel began.

But the moment I placed the receiver on the cradle, the phone began to ring again, and again I snatched it up.

"Chaplain Jordan," I said.

"Can you talk?" the kidnapper asked.

"Yes. Give me just a second."

Rachel stood. "I'll let you take that, go see what the warden wants. Be back in a few."

"Thanks," I said.

I noticed she had removed the recorder from my desk, but wasn't holding it as she started to leave.

I stood and walked around the desk, never letting go of the receiver. She had left the recorder on and placed it on the floor at the base of my desk.

I reached down, snatched it up, and tossed it to her.

"It must have fallen when I tried to put it in my pocket," she said.

"Must have," I said, my voice revealing far more incredulity than hers had before. "Miraculously, hitting the floor didn't disengage the recording mechanism."

She gave me a wry smile and was out the door.

"I'm here," I said to the caller.

"What am I interrupting?" he asked.

"Nothing. I've been waiting for your call."

"No, I mean what were you doing when I called?"

"Being interviewed by the inspector about my involvement in the death of a staff member that happened here a few days ago," I said.

"Is it a problem?"

"No."

"Is he gone?"

"Yes," I said, not correcting his assumption.

He knew how to reach me in the chapel at the prison but didn't know the new IG was a woman. What else did he know and not know?

"Have you spoken to anyone about anything?"

"Absolutely not. I've done exactly what you've told me to. Nothing more. Nothing less. How is Anna?"

"She's good. Resting. We're taking better care of her than you did. I assure you. The only thing that can go wrong with any of this, the only way she gets mistreated or dead, is if you do something I've told you not to or fuck up something I've told you to do."

"Not gonna happen," I said. "Can I speak to her?"

"I told you, she's sleeping. You'll talk to her again soon. And if you do what I tell you, you'll see her tomorrow night."

"Okay. Who am I bringing you to trade for her?"

"Last name is Cardigan," he said. "Like the sweater. First name Ronnie. DC number 745491. You have a little over a day. Make it count."

Chapter Seventeen

I had a name.

Now I had to come up with a plan.

And I had a day to do it.

The first thing I did was call down to Classification and request Cardigan's file.

While waiting for the inmate jacket to arrive, I called around to find out what job and dorm Ronnie was assigned to.

Previously, everything I was doing now was accomplished with a single phone call to Anna.

That thought made me even more sad and lonely, and for a moment I was overcome with such intense longing, I couldn't catch my breath.

No time for that now. Put it away. No good to her if you don't.

I took a moment, gathered myself, and once again returned to the place deep inside, distancing myself from all else.

Thoughts that do often lie too deep for tears.

Wordsworth's line came to mind, and I made myself concentrate on the verse, actually saying it out loud in my empty office.

""Thanks to the human heart by which we live.

Thanks to its tenderness, its joys, and its fears. To me the
meanest flower that blows can give, Thoughts that do often
lie too deep for tears.'"

That's where I've got to be, to get back to, to stay
until I get Anna back—in the place where my thoughts lie
too deep for tears.

The file was delivered to my desk in a stringed state
courier envelope by an inmate orderly from Classification
before I had finished my calls. I flipped through it while
I was on the phone, and by the time Ronnie reached my
office, I knew a good bit about him.

Serving a ridiculous mandatory minimum on a
nonviolent possession-with-intent-to-distribute charge, he
had been failed by his public defender, and had a lot of
time left on his sentence. A model inmate, he was housed
in the honor dorm, and worked in the kitchen as a cook. A
constant reader, he used the library as much as any inmate
on the compound. A devout Catholic, he never missed
Mass.

Cardigan looked like someone who would wear one.

As if a community college professor instead of a
state of Florida inmate, Ronnie Cardigan blinked a lot
behind his big glasses and wore his coarse light-brown-
going-gray hair as long as the prison would allow, combing
it back into a soft, full white man's low afro. His body was a
bit bulky—not fat, but broad and soft.

"You know why you're here?" I asked.

"Oh, God, no. My mom? Please tell me she didn't
die."

I shook my head. "No. Nothing like that. Sorry to

alarm you."

"Oh, thank God. I'm so . . . so relieved. Thank God. Thank you God."

"I thought you would know."

"Know what?"

"Why you're here."

"Why would I?" he asked.

"Have you spoken with your family lately?"

He shook his head. "Usually call once during the weekends. Missed 'em last weekend. Won't call again until this one coming up. Do you know why I was denied a furlough? That somethin' you could help me with? I'm in on a nonviolent charge. I've never gotten a single DR. They say the reason I can't go is I've got too much time left on my sentence."

I considered him carefully. He seemed genuine, and seemed to genuinely have no idea what was going on. But his big glasses, nearly constant blinking, and his avoidance of eye contact made him difficult to read.

"I'll see what I can do," I said.

"Just want to see my mom before she . . . before it's too late."

I began to formulate a plan. Tomorrow night one of our volunteers would be in the chapel facilitating a Bible study group. If I could get Ronnie to join the other inmates in attendance . . .

"How badly do you want to see her?"

He looked confused. "Bad."

If I could get approval for another volunteer to come in . . . One that resembled Ronnie . . .

"What would you do to get to see her?" I asked.

"Anything."

"*Anything*?" I asked.

"I mean it. Anything."

"Serve more time?"

He nodded. "In a heartbeat. I'm tellin' you, anything. Sayin' bye on the phone just isn't. . . That's not how I want to . . . say what all I want to say."

I nodded. "I understand."

"Chaplain, why am I here?"

"I know you're Catholic, but I'd like you to attend the Protestant study group tomorrow night."

He looked confused, but said, "Okay."

"It's very important. I really need you here."

He nodded. "Okay. But I'm not going to convert."

"Nothing like that," I said. "And I want you to call your family before you come. Either tonight or tomorrow but before you come to the study. Okay? It's important. Both are. Call your family and be here for the study."

Chapter Eighteen

Which of my volunteers looked the most like Ronnie Cardigan?

What if none of them resembled him at all?

To be a chapel volunteer at PCI, you had to undergo an extensive background check, a training program, and be issued a photo ID, which had to be presented to the control room officer upon entering and exiting the institution.

Did I have anyone who was already approved who looked anything like Cardigan?

There was a religious professor from FSU who came occasionally who reminded me of Cardigan, but there was very little physical resemblance between them.

Most of the volunteers we had were senior citizens. The others were either female, ethnic or the wrong race, or just weren't even close in appearance.

What if I didn't use one of our existing volunteers?

Under certain circumstances for one-time special programs, we could run a background check on a potential volunteer and the warden could approve him or her to enter the institution under the supervision of the chaplain.

Who did I know who looked like Cardigan?

If I could find someone . . .

How would I . . . ?

If I could find someone who resembled Cardigan, get him approved, bring him into the chapel, drug him, call Cardigan into my office, switch their clothes . . . I'd still have to get past the control room with him, but . . . it might work. But who?

"You pray a lot," Rachel Peterson said.

I turned around to see her standing about halfway down the center aisle.

"Guilty conscience?"

"No more than reason," I said.

"What does that—"

"Shakespeare," I said.

"Oh."

"Ready to continue?" I asked.

"We feel it's best if you're placed on nonadministrative leave while we conduct the investigation," she said.

Heart raising. Heat emanating. Breath catching.

A hole opened inside me and everything slid down into it.

I had just come up with a plan to save Anna that could possibly work, and was now being told I wouldn't be here to even attempt it.

"We?" I asked, trying to get my bearings.

"The warden. Me. The regional chaplain."

"I'm the only chaplain on duty," I said. "I have several services to supervise. I'm in the middle of some very intense crisis counseling situations. I really need to be here."

"The warden said he'd call the staff chaplain back in. The regional chaplain said he'd get everything covered or come do it himself if he needed to."

"Just to get rid of me," I said. "Wow. I've never been

so unwanted anywhere."

"Maybe it means you should think about doing something else."

"Maybe so," I said. "As far as the investigation you're conducting . . . I did nothing wrong."

"Nothing?"

"I'm . . . I mean . . . whoever gave the order to fire on the inmate in the quad is responsible for Hahn's death."

"That's what my investigation will determine," she said.

"Appears to be *pre*determined," I said.

"It's not."

"Then answer this for me," I said. "Who else is being put on administrative leave? The shooter? The response team leader? The inspector?"

She didn't say anything but her expression said it all.

"That's what I thought," I said.

T*hree men.*

There are three, but are they all men? They are.

Why do you think that?

It's just the sense I get. Like everything else. It's movement and smell and . . . what . . . intuition.

Three men taking very good care of me.

One young. The talker. The early twenties one with the resonate voice.

One older. The rarely speaks one. The one that smells like . . . what? Some kind of common cologne and . . . gum. Chewing gum. Not bubble gum. Minty old-school chewing gum in the small, inexpensive packs. With foil.

Something about him reminds her of someone from the prison, but who?

She thinks about it, but can't come up with anyone in particular.

But what about the third one. The one she wasn't sure existed until now. The silent, distant, shadow one.

A random refrain of oppressive organ music from the old Shadow radio show echoed through her mind.

Who knows what evil lurks in the hearts of men?

The Shadow knows.

I'm gonna know . . . eventually. And so is John.

Is the Shadow in charge? Calling the shots? Why doesn't he speak? Is he unable to? Or is he just a man of few words? Are the three equals? In this together?

Or is the talker in charge? Why do I think he's not? Because he's so young? No, there's something else. What is it?

Before she could come up with it, he stepped over to her and said, "Here. Take this."

He untied one of her wrists and handed her a pill.

"What is it?"

"You wouldn't believe me if I told you," he said.

"Try me."

"A prenatal vitamin."

"You're right. I don't believe you."

"And you don't have to. But you do have to take it. So . . ."

She popped the pill into her mouth and he handed her a glass. Tilting her head back, she took a swallow of the liquid—orange juice, actually—and swallowed the pill.

"It really is a prenatal vitamin," he said. "We want you and your baby healthy and in perfect condition when we return you to John."

"When will that be?"

"Won't be long now," he said. "Unless he fucks it up, won't be long at all."

Chapter Nineteen

Now what?

I had no idea what to do.

I couldn't very well get Ronnie Cardigan out of the prison if I couldn't even get into it.

I was truly lost.

Anna's life was on the line. Time was running out. And the nearly impossible task before me had just become completely impossible.

When Randy Wayne Davis, the youngish control room sergeant with the bright blue eyes and bright white teeth, buzzed me into the sally port between the first of the two front gates, he motioned me over to the inside control room document tray.

"How's it going, Chaplain?"

Not even the thick glass or the dark tint on it could diminish his bright, wide eyes and infectious smile.

I nodded without answering, leaned over so that my mouth was closer to the open document tray, and said, "How are you?"

"I'm good. Hey, I just transferred a call down to the chapel for you. You headed up front? Want me to transfer it to the warden's office if they call back?"

I thought about it. I started to tell him what was going on and how to actually handle my calls, but decided it'd be best if he didn't know—especially if I tried to sneak back into the institution the next night.

"Sure," I said. "Thanks."

"You got it."

I started to walk away, but he said, "And hey, just wanted to say . . . All the good you do around here—for the staff as well as the inmates—doesn't go unnoticed."

That put a knot in my throat and a sting in my eyes.

"Thank you, Sergeant Davis. That really—"

"Randy Wayne, please."

I nodded and started to say his name, but the phone in the control room rang and he said, "Hold on a second. Let me see if this is them callin' back for you."

I waited as he answered the phone.

When it took more than a few seconds I knew it wasn't for me, but after talking to the caller for nearly two minutes, Randy Wayne fed the phone through the document tray for me.

"Sorry," he said with a frown.

"Don't know what's taking so long up there," Rachel Peterson's voice said across the line, "but I've informed the sergeant of your status and told him you need to exit the institution immediately."

When I handed Randy Wayne the phone, he shook his head. "That's not right," he said. "Everybody knows what happened down there and who's responsible."

"Thanks."

"Wait," he said, his big blue eyes getting even bigger, "I may know someone who might be able to help."

I was desperate. I'd take anything.

"Give me your cell number and I'll call you after I do a little . . . after I make a few calls."

"How are the plans and arrangements coming along?"

I was out driving around thinking, because I didn't know what else to do and I loved driving Anna's Mustang, when the call came.

"I'm working on them," I said. "Everything will—"

"Why aren't you in your office?"

How does he know I'm not?

"Sounds like you're driving," he said.

"I'm working on the plan. Driving around thinking."

"Not headed somewhere private to tell the authorities about all this?"

"No. Absolutely not."

"Swear?" he said. "On her life? 'Cause that's what it is. Her life."

"I know that."

"I told you to keep everything as normal as possible."

"I am. I'm on my lunch break. I often drive around and think."

"Not today. I want you back at the institution."

"Okay, I've got to do something first, but then I'll head back."

"What? What do you have to do first? I wouldn't think you'd be so reckless with your wife's life."

Wife again. Does he really think she is?

"My mom died last week. I was supposed to have already picked out the image and quote for her headstone. I promised I'd do it no later than today. It won't take too long but I've already promised to meet the guy doing it."

"Hurry then. And if you're lying, it's her life."

"Can I speak to her?"

"I'll call in an hour. If you're back at the prison, you can talk to her."

I dropped the phone in the passenger seat, not knowing what to do. All I had done was buy a little time. Very little. What could I do with it?

I gunned the engine and sped down the rural route of the flat, pine tree–lined highway, racing nowhere fast.

How can I get back into the institution?

I thought about it.

There was nothing I could do. Nothing to—

I could make up an excuse, something left behind in my office that I needed.

They'd never go for that—and even if they did, it wouldn't get me back inside long enough to really help. And it didn't address the most important problem—being there tomorrow night to get Cardigan out.

I could ask for mercy from the warden.

But he had none, not for me.

I could make a deal with the warden. Agree to resign at the end of the week if he'd just let me come back and finish out the week.

That might work. It would certainly appeal to him. But . . . would he go for it?

Probably not. Especially when he thinks the investigation into Hahn's death will get me out anyway.

What if an inmate's wife with an emergency demanded to speak to me? Or a volunteer?

I doubted even that would work.

What I had told the kidnapper was partially true. I had yet to select an image and quote for Mom's headstone. Today was not the deadline, though. That had been the lie.

But when I became aware of where I was, I realized I was coming up on Whispering Pines Lane, the road that led to the cemetery. I slowed, tapped the blinker on, and turned down the road we all travel alone.

Had my subconscious brought me here? Before or after what I had said to the caller?

I parked as close to her graveside as I could, got out, and walked over the fall-browning grass toward her empty headstone, wondering if winter's first green is gold, what is fall's first brown.

Most of the flower arrangements left from the funeral were dead or nearly dead, many of the white plastic baskets tipped over.

I bent down and straightened them.

Close to the earth, touching the dead and dying flowers, my mom's decaying body just six feet beyond. *Thoughts that do often lie too deep for tears.*

"I'm sorry I haven't been by to see you sooner," I said.

The shade from a nearby tree fell just short of her new grave, the midday sun causing the granite of the gravestone and the sandy soil of the fill dirt to gleam brightly.

The bareness of her headstone looked bad, unfinished, as if she were uncared for, which was not the case.

"I'm sorry about your headstone too. I'll get to it soon. I swear. "

I swear is not something I normally say, and I wondered if it was me reverting back to a more juvenile state while talking to my dead mother or my conversation with the kidnapper.

"I miss you far more than I ever thought I would," I said. "Didn't realize how much good the visits I thought I was doing for you were actually doing for me."

In the far corner of the cemetery, a large, old car rattled up to a stop, and a short, stocky elderly man with a felt hat and overcoat stumbled out and lumbered over to a cement bench next to a double headstone.

"I've got to go, Mom," I said, "but I'll be back soon. And I'll get your marker done. I promise. I love you. Miss you."

I lingered for a moment more then made my way back to Anna's car, walking not unlike the elderly man on the backside of the cemetery had.

Chapter Twenty

I drove home with an overwhelming sense of dread.

Whether from my visit to my Mom's grave or being locked out of the prison, I felt a futility like I hadn't in a very long time, and I wondered if I'd ever see Anna alive again.

Can't think like that. Push it down. Put it away. Focus on figuring out how to do what you need to do. Nothing else.

Nothing else.

At home the first thing I did was go to the small bedroom Anna and I had been sharing for such a short time.

Sitting on her side of the bed, I picked up the book she had been reading for the few minutes she could stay wake each night after coming to bed. She had always had difficulty staying up late—something her pregnancy had kicked into overdrive.

Lifting the top book, *Ultimate Crime Ultimate Punishment*, a law text on the death penalty, it revealed a smaller book beneath it—*A Good Divorce, A Good Marriage*.

I knew she had been reading the law book. Though she wasn't practicing and wasn't sure she would, Anna had recently graduated from FSU Law School and was fascinated with all things criminal justice. With the upheaval in her life, and being with child, I knew it was too much for her to think about just now, but I hoped one day she would practice law, because I knew how good she would be at it.

I hadn't known she was also reading the relationship book. But it didn't surprise me. Not at all. Of course she would want to have the best divorce possible. Of course she would want us to have the best relationship possible. Of course she would do all she could to make both of those things happen.

I wondered if the experience of being shot and almost dying and the possibility of Anna never coming back to him would change Chris at all. He obviously cared about her. Could he get past the rejection and blow to his ego that her leaving him was? Would he ever take responsibility for his affairs and mistreatment of her?

It's all moot if you don't get her back.

Placing the books back just like they had been, I laid my head on her pillow and breathed her in, the smell of her shampoo and perfume creating an olfactory experience that simultaneously heightened both her presence and absence here.

I missed her so much. I was so tired, so sleepy, so spent in every way, I wanted to stay here like this, drift into the gentle oblivion of unconsciousness with the sweet smell of her swirling around me, but I forced myself to get up and do what I came home to do.

Going into the little living room, where on every wall were stacks of my books, I got pen and paper and wrote a note explaining everything to Merrill and asking him to square things if I failed to.

A certain hollowed-out hopelessness still sat at my center, but writing the letter—having someone like Merrill to write it to—made me feel better.

When I opened my front door to leave, I saw, to my surprise, Chris Taunton easing into the yard in a car I didn't recognize.

He pulled in sideways, placing the vehicle perpendicular to the trailer, and rolled his window down.

"Don't make me try to get out," he said.

"The hell are you doing?" I asked.

He was leaned way back in the seat, sitting stiff and gingerly, and looked a half step above dead. When he reached up to put the car in park, he winced in pain.

"Something against doctor's orders," he said, "but I want to help you find her and get her back. I have to."

"You're jeopardizing her life just by being here. What if they see you? What could you do to help anyway?"

"I can't lay there thinking about all the ways I did her wrong."

"Maybe that's exactly what you need to be doing."

"Punish myself? For how long? The rest of my life?"

"No. Reflect. Repent. Learn."

"Repent? I've already asked God to forgive me a thousand times."

"Means nothing. I'm talking about making changes. Repent means to go in a different direction."

"That's what I'm trying to do. By the way, what happened to my car? You seen it?"

My phone rang.

I held up my hand and gave him a look that said be quiet.

"Are you back at the prison?" the caller asked.

Would you know if I wasn't?

"Nearly."

"Nearly isn't good enough, John. Not nearly good enough."

"I will be soon."

"Why aren't you following my instructions? Don't tell me I overestimated your care for your wife."

Chris mouthed, *What is he saying?*

"You did not. I'm trying to do everything you asked. Just like you want it done."

"Doesn't seem that way to me," he said. "I want this to have a happy ending for all of us, but I'm not playing games, not making idle threats. You saw what we did to the guy who tried to be a hero. Don't make me kill her. I honestly don't want to. But know this—I will if I have to. Then I will find someone else to do what I need done. Understand?"

"I do."

"I will call you again in fifteen minutes. You better be back at the prison."

"I will be."

I hung up.

"I've got to go," I said to Chris. "You need to go back to the hospital. If there's anything you can do I will let you know. But for now, you can't be seen."

I didn't wait for him to respond. Just jumped into Anna's Mustang and sped away.

Chapter Twenty-one

As I raced toward the prison, I tried to formulate a plan for getting back in.

I kept coming up short, but the irony of going from working so hard to figure how to break an inmate out to now trying to devise a plan to break back in wasn't lost on me.

At a minimum I would be at the prison when the kidnapper called back. I could go inside the admin or training buildings, which were outside the fence, if nothing else. If anyone asked what I was doing, I could say I came back because I wanted to meet with the warden about my future.

Of course, I'd be surprised if anybody but Randy Wayne, the warden and maybe his secretary even knew anything about my suspension.

I arrived at the institution with one minute to spare.

The warden's office was on the far left side of the admin building closest to the front gate of the prison, so I entered through the front door on the opposite end, something mostly only visitors did, and was greeted by Brandy Jean Bateman, the buxom blonde with perpetual relationship dilemmas, who was forever soliciting advice she never took.

"Just the man I wanted to see," she said. "I've got a question for you."

"I'll be right back to answer it for you, but I have to run take care of something first."

"Sure," she said, sighing with a certain wistful resignation, as if all men made her wait. "Take your time. I'll be here."

I rushed past her as my phone started ringing.

Answering it as quickly as I could, I ducked into the Mens to take it.

"Are you back at the prison?"

"I am," I said, entering the first of the two small stalls and closing the door.

"What's that echo?"

"You really want to know?" I asked, trying to think of something to say.

"Wouldn't've asked if I didn't."

"I'm in the restroom. All this has my stomach messed up."

"Sorry," he said, and he sounded liked he meant it, "this will all be over soon."

"Speaking to Anna will help."

"Here she is."

"John?" Anna said.

"Are you okay?"

"I'm fine. I really am. I just miss you so much. They're treating me very well. All I need in the world is to be back with you . . . and a nice long bath."

"You'll have both very soon. I'm gonna get you out of there."

"I know how you are," she said. "But take care of yourself too. Not just me and everybody else. Are you eating? Have you slept any at all?"

"I'm okay. I'll be great as soon as you're back safe

and sound."

"I love you so much," she said.

"I love you. See you soon."

There was a rustling sound on the phone and she was gone.

"Why are you risking your wife's life, John?" the kidnapper asked.

"What?"

"I told you to do exactly what I say and not to ever lie to me."

"I—"

"Why would you tell me you're at the prison when you're—"

"I am. I told you."

"You lied."

"I didn't."

"You're not there."

"I told you," I said. "My stomach is . . . I had a . . . an emergency. As soon as I got back, I ran into the closest bathroom. I'm in the men's restroom in Admin right now. It's where I've been since the moment I got back."

"I meant for you to be in your office. In the chapel."

"I will be. I just had to—"

"You better not be lying, John."

With that he ended the call.

"What the *hell* are *you* doin' here?"

As I pulled the restroom door open and stepped out, I walked into the warden.

Anger reddened his fleshy face, flared his nostrils, furrowed his brow.

Bat Matson was a man who expected to be obeyed.

"Answer me," he said, his jowls shaking a bit as he did.

"I asked him to join us," Carrie Helms said.

I turned to see Helms, Randy Wayne Davis, and Pine Tree Peavey walking down the narrow hallway toward us.

Carrie Helms was in front, Randy not far behind her, Pine lumbering after them, eclipsing everything behind him.

Pete Pine Tree Peavey was the largest man I'd ever seen in person. Not just tall, but wide, he wasn't a narrow, quick-growing slash pine but a massive, thick-bodied loblolly pine.

"*Us*? Who? The chaplain is on suspension."

"He won't be after you hear what Pi—Sergeant Peavey has to say," Randy Wayne said, adding, as if an afterthought, a subtle smartass "Sir."

"He's an eyewitness," Carrie said.

"To what?" Matson asked.

"What happened in H Dorm the night Ms. Ling was killed," Pine said. "I was on duty. Saw the whole thing."

"My office," Matson said. "I'll be there in a minute. Sergeant Davis, tell Crystal to call Inspector Peterson and tell her to meet us there."

Matson entered the restroom and the rest of us headed toward his office, Pine in front now.

"Think you'd ever see a cavalry that looked like the four of us?" Carrie asked.

"You literally can't see anything on the other side of him," Randy Wayne, who was right behind Pine, was saying.

"Four?" I said.

Carrie and Randy Wayne started laughing.

"Yeah," she said. "Merrill's on the other side of Pine."

Merrill, Carrie, Randy Wayne, Pine, Rachel Peterson, and I were all crowded into Matson's office.

Of course, had it just been Pine, it would've still been crowded.

"What's this about?" Rachel asked.

"That's what we're here to find out," Matson said.

"We don't understand why Chaplain Jordan has been suspended," Randy Wayne said. "Sergeant Monroe corroborated his account of what happened in H Dorm the night Hahn was killed."

"Let's just say we're not sure Sergeant Monroe is the most reliable witness where his best friend, the chaplain, is concerned," Rachel said.

"Well, how about the sergeant who was on duty in the dorm that night?" Carrie said.

"I assume you mean Sergeant Peavey," she said.

"I do."

"Are you a good friend of the chaplain's too?" Rachel asked.

"Barely know him at all," Pine said. "I know of him. We both grew up here, but he's at least ten years older than me, so we really didn't even go to school together, and—"

"I was being facetious," she said.

"Oh."

"Give us your account of what happened in H Dorm the night Hahn Ling was killed," Rachel said, snapping on her recorder and holding it out toward him.

He did.

And it matched what Merrill and I had already told her.

"Did anyone coach you on what to say?" she asked.

"No, ma'am."

"Not in any way?"

"I was just called up here from the compound," he said. "Had no idea what was going on."

Rachel looked at Matson. He frowned and shrugged. "Think maybe you should've spoken with the officers on duty in the dorm that night before suspending the chaplain?" he said.

"The suspension was your idea," she said.

"Based on what you told me your investigation was revealing," he said.

She shook her head and sighed.

As if suddenly realizing we were all still in the room, Matson looked at us and said, "Get back to work. All of you. You too, Chaplain."

Chapter Twenty-two

"Thank you," I said to Carrie as we walked from the admin building toward the control room.

"Thank Randy Wayne. It was all him."

"Thank you," I said to him. "Thank you all."

He and Pine, who were a few steps in front of us, slowed and turned.

"Just did what was right," Randy Wayne said. "I hate a bully. The new warden's a bully. And you do so much good around here, Chaplain. And I don't ever see anyone thanking you."

"Thank you," I said again.

When they turned back around, Carrie Helms lowered her rough, scratchy voice and said, "What can you tell me about what happened to Chris Taunton? I heard he was dead. Shot to death."

That afternoon I counseled with an officer whose wife was leaving him.

"She says I'm a different person from the one she married," he said.

He was a meek and mild-mannered young man with

closely cropped brown hair and sad, sagging brown eyes.

"Says working here has changed me."

It probably had. It was a difficult job in an inhumane environment, a daily assault on civility and humanity. Incidences of alcohol and drug abuse, depression, anxiety, and domestic violence all increased among correctional officers.

"Has it?" I asked.

He seemed to think about it for a moment, then frowned, shrugged, and nodded. "Yeah, guess it has."

"It's a dark, difficult place," I said.

"But . . . our vows were for better or worse."

"How much worse is it?" I asked.

He didn't respond right away.

My mind kept wanting to wander back to Anna, to the plan and preparations, and I had to keep bringing it back to this moment, to helping this man, to being present—something I was finding challenging in the midst of everything else I was doing these days.

"It's not bad all the time," he said. "But . . . I do have a shorter fuse these days. I don't know, it's like I'm always on edge. Sometimes I just lose it. Definitely drink too much. Not sure what all I do to her when I . . . when I'm drinking."

"Have you hit her?"

"No. Nothing like that. I wouldn't blame her for leavin' if I ever did anything like that. And I won't."

We talked for a long time after that, but the more he talked the more futile it all felt. It wasn't that he couldn't make the monumental, fundamental changes needed to save his marriage. It was that, like most of us, he *wouldn't* make them. He wanted *things* to change, but there are no things. There is only us. We change us—our thoughts, words, and deeds—or we change nothing.

Later in the afternoon, I supervised an inmate AA group—something I always found difficult to do.

The meeting was held in one corner of the chow hall. Open and airy and full of hard concrete and metal surfaces, the coffee- and cigarette-laced breath of the words spoken by the inmates ricocheted around the room and were gone, lost like everything else they had ever had.

I felt awkward when placed in the position of being present in a meeting I was facilitating but not participating in.

It felt dishonest not to tell the inmates attending that I too was a friend of Bill W's, and that the program that works if you work it had worked for me, *was* working for me. But there were inmates who exploited any personal information they could obtain about officers and staff, and I couldn't run the risk of being compromised in a way that prevented me from effectively serving my parish. Still, it made me feel like a liar.

Fortunately, it wasn't something that happened all that often. I only supervised the group when Lee Friedman, the volunteer sponsor, was unable to do it.

Today's meeting was designated as a step meeting, so over bad coffee in light blue plastic cups, the incarcerated men in various stages of recovery discussed how to make a searching and fearless moral inventory of themselves.

As they did, I thought about how brilliant and elegant the twelve steps were.

Of the few things I would even consider to possibly be truly inspired, these simple, proven, life-changing steps were certainly among them.

This thought led inevitably to others, and before long I was constructing a list of the writings I considered to be canonical—poetry and narrative I considered to contain the breath of God.

But before I ever completed my list of sacred texts, the meeting came to a close, ending with all of us standing in a circle saying aloud, "God grant me the serenity to accept the things I cannot change, courage to change the things I can, and the wisdom to know the difference. One day at a time. Keep coming back. It works if you work it."

When I reached Anna's car at the end of the day, Jake was waiting for me.

It was nearly an hour after the admin shift had ended, the parking lot largely empty, my coworkers long gone. We were alone.

"I owe you," Jake said. "So I ain't gonna ask what you're using this for, but I can't think of anything good you could be doin' with it."

I nodded.

"You sure about this?"

I nodded again.

"Is it something I can help you with?" he asked.

I shook my head. "Thank you, though. That means a lot."

"Okay," he said, frowning and shaking his head.

He withdrew a small clear vile from the pocket of his green deputy's uniform pants and handed it to me.

"You're doing it here?" I asked in surprise, quickly tucking the vile in the pocket of my suit coat. "Like this?"

"John, no one thinks a sheriff's deputy and a chaplain are doin' a drug deal in the prison parkin' lot."

"What is it?" I asked.

"What you asked for. An incapacitation and memory loss agent. Date rape drug. Either rohypnol or ketamine. It'll put whoever you give it to in a trance state or actually sedate them and they won't remember it."

I wondered if he got it out of the evidence room or off the street, but didn't ask. "And you're sure it works, it's—"

"It works like a motherfucker. It's powerful and potent and I wish there wasn't stuff like it in the world."

"Okay. Thanks."

"What the fuck are you up to, John?"

"I'll tell you when I can. I promise."

"Okay. You and Dad are the only two people on the planet I'd do something like this for."

"I know. I really appreciate it."

"Be careful," he said. "I'm just getting to where I kinda like your odd ass."

It was the nicest thing he had said to me since we were children, and I stepped forward and hugged him.

"The fuck you doin'?" he said, but he hugged me back a bit, then pushed me away.

Chapter Twenty-three

My entire plan hinged on this.

I was in the warden's office first thing the next morning following another mostly sleepless night, with a special request for Emmitt Emerson to enter the institution as a one-time volunteer to speak at the Christian worship service in the chapel later in the day.

"I've heard about this young man," Matson said. "Very impressive. Powerful testimony. Now see, this is the kind of thing I like to take place in my prison. This is the kind of program I've been askin' you to do. Gives me hope. Maybe this most recent scare about your job did you some good."

I just listened and nodded, didn't say anything.

I should've known he would have heard of Emmitt Emerson, a former high school football star who had spent all his time since graduating drinking, doing drugs, and having sex with girls who were still in school, who had recently undergone a dramatic conversion experience for which he was receiving lots of attention.

In addition to speaking at virtually every church in the Panhandle, Emerson had been on nearly all the local radio and TV shows telling how he should be dead but God had a greater plan for his life, and hawking the small, poorly written self-published paperback with the bad cover that told his story, or as he and Matson would call it, his testimony.

When it had occurred to me just how much Emmitt Emerson looked like Ronnie Cardigan, I too became a believer. God did have a greater plan for Emmitt's life—helping me get Anna back.

"This will do the inmates some real good," Matson was saying. "To see a young man not unlike themselves saved by the grace of God, to hear how he was going down the same path as many of them . . ."

He signed his approval on the memo granting Emerson permission to enter the prison with a large looping signature, as if he were as proud to do so as John Hancock was the Declaration of Independence.

This was far easier than I had ever dreamed. Emerson was not only available but grateful for the opportunity to come in and speak to the men, and Matson was only too happy to let him.

Now if only every other aspect of the plan could come off as smoothly.

"What time will he speak?" Matson asked. "I'd like to come hear him."

For a moment I lost the capacity for speech.

Shit. Think fast.

"Seven-thirty," I said. "But . . ."

"But what?"

"It's just . . . I really want the men to get all they can out of the service."

"Yeah?"

"I think having the warden there might make them distracted, self-conscious. In the past, any time a dignitary has attended a service, the men are so interested in watching him or impressing him that they miss the real meaning of the . . ."

He liked being referred to as a dignitary.

"How would we know if those who respond to the altar call aren't just doing it to impress you?" I said.

"I never want to hinder the work of God," he said.

"I've got an idea," I said.

"What's that?"

"What if I invite Evangelist Emerson to speak to the staff?" I said. "He could be a special guest speaker at the luncheon devotional I do on Thursdays."

"That's a God-inspired idea, Chaplain," he said.

He had never attended the inspirational luncheon I conducted every Thursday in the fellowship hall, and I had heard he had discouraged the staff from doing so, but my guess is he would not only not miss this one, but he'd make it an unspoken but very much implied mandatory event for all staff on Admin shift—the only ones to get an hour lunch break.

"I don't know what's gotten into you, Chaplain, but I like it. Keep it up. Keep it up. See when Reverend Emerson can attend and set it up. Let me know the moment you do so I can let the staff know I expect them to attend."

He's not even going to be subtle about it.

"Will do."

"And keep up the good work. More of this. Less doing my inspector's work. You just might have a future here."

I smiled at the irony.

By doing this—whether it succeeded or failed—I was guaranteeing I would have absolutely no future here at all.

"Speaking of the future," he said. "Do you know what tonight is? A blood moon. 'And I beheld when he had opened the sixth seal, and, lo, there was a great earthquake; and the sun became black as sackcloth of hair, and the moon became as blood.'"

I nodded.

"Tonight's not just any blood moon, though," he said. "It's the end of a tetrad—four consecutive blood moons that coincide with Jewish holidays with six full moons in between. We're witnessing the unfolding of biblical prophecy. A sign of End Times."

I wasn't able to nod at that. I had a low tolerance for ignorance and superstition and the vanity and egocentricity that made every generation believe it was the final and most significant. It's a vain generation that seeks a sign.

"That's what Emmitt Emerson is speaking on tonight."

Chapter Twenty-four

Everything was ready.

Now all that was left was for me to wait and question what I was about to do, obsessing over every detail.

Which is what I was doing in the chapel when Rachel Peterson came in.

"I said you prayed a lot, but what I meant was you're the most praying person I know."

I shrugged and laughed. "I doubt that. Guess it depends on how you define it. For me, prayer is everything."

"Obviously," she said, her green-gray eyes widening. "You certainly do a lot of it."

"No, I meant everything is prayer."

"Huh?"

"Wasn't saying prayer is everything. Was saying everything is prayer."

"Oh," she said. "So if you were in here thinking about . . . I don't know . . . sports or . . . your laundry . . . or lusting after a coworker . . . that would be prayer?"

"Could be."

She nodded. "Well, anyway, I was just about to leave and I thought . . . I don't know, that maybe I owe you some sort of an apology."

"Well, most any sort is prayer," I said with a smile.

"Even the begrudging sort?" she said with a big, beautiful, widemouthed smile of her own.

"Especially."

"I'm not sure about you," she said. "But you're interesting as hell, I'll give you that. And I think, given the chance, I'd enjoy working a case with you one day."

"Maybe we will."

"Maybe."

"Is your investigation into Hahn's death complete?"

She shook her head. "Getting there, though."

"Do you know who took the shot?"

She nodded.

"Did he do it on his own or was he ordered to?"

"Pray about it," she said. "I'm sure it'll come to you."

"Are you going to make sure Hahn gets justice?"

"Too late for that," she said. "But I'm gonna get the bastard who shot the man who was holding her life in his hands."

After Rachel left, I went over everything again. Step by step. Move by move. Trying to examine all the moving parts and evaluate all the eventualities.

What was I forgetting? What hadn't I thought of?

Is there another way?

Even at this late date, this far in, I wondered if there were any other options.

I was taking actions that would free a Florida state inmate, cost me my career, send me to jail, and possibly get people hurt or killed.

Anna was worth it. Anna was worth everything. But

was there another way? One that would still save her and not risk her life? I couldn't think of one.

What would happen if I showed up without Cardigan? Would they kill her on the spot? Give me the chance to explain?

What if I had the meeting place surrounded? Would they be spotted? Would they not show? Drive away? Kill her?

I couldn't risk it. I couldn't do anything that would risk her life. I had to do everything I could to get her back—no matter the risks involved, no matter the costs.

I cared about my career, my calling. Cared deeply. I cared about doing my job, about keeping the public safe, keeping inmates in custody. I cared about all of it. But compared to Anna, I didn't care at all. By comparison I couldn't care less.

No, there were no other options. Nothing to do but what I was doing. It was immoral and illegal and insane.

The phone in my office rang.

I had left the door connecting my office with the chapel open so I could hear it.

I quickly climbed to my feet and rushed over to answer it.

"Chaplain Jordan."

"That's more like it," the kidnapper said. "Welcome back."

Was he just saying that because I wasn't here yesterday when he called, or did he know I had been suspended?

"Whatta you mean?"

"Are you ready?" he said, ignoring my question.

"I am. Everything is set. Just tell me where to meet you."

"We'll get to that. First, let me remind you of

something. It's very important. I honestly and truly only want to make the trade. I will not double-cross you. I will not hurt you or the girl. Unless you force me to. Understand? Do just as I tell you and you will get her back tonight and we'll all walk away with what we want. I mean it. Her fate as well as your own is in your hands. It's very simple. Don't try to be a hero. Don't do anything but what I tell you to do. Please."

"That's all I've been doing. That's all I'll do. She means too much to me to . . . risk something happening to her."

"Okay then."

"Best to remember that," I said. "If I do what you tell me to and something happens to her, I will come after you. Me and every cop and criminal and sadistic motherfucker I know."

"Wow. I'm really surprised to hear a chaplain talk that way."

"Just want you to know how serious I am," I said. "Wanted it to stick in your head. Wanted you to understand."

"I do. I think we understand each other. So let's do this."

"When and where?"

"You say the when, I'll say the where."

I thought about it. "As long as the drive is not too far, seven-thirty."

"Perfect. In the woods on the east side of the institution—between the prison and Potter Farm, where the girl was killed a little while back. Know where I mean?"

"I do."

"There's a path that leads by a pond that runs all the way through—from the backside of Potter Farm to the end of the woods where the clearing of the prison property starts. Walk that path with the inmate. I'll meet you somewhere along it. I'll have the girl. You won't know where. Got it?"

"Got it."

"And John, I've had people watching it for days. If you try to send anyone in to set up to capture or kill me, I'll know. Don't try anything. Understand?"

"I do. And you should understand something too. If you call Anna a girl again, I'll have to kill you on principle alone."

Chapter Twenty-five

Emmitt Emerson used to be an obnoxious, self-centered, narrow-minded, drug-addicted, shallow asshole.

Then he was born again.

Now he was a born again obnoxious, self-centered, narrow-minded, religion-addicted, shallow asshole.

I had met him at the front gate and was now being helped by Randy Wayne Davis to get him signed in and through the sally port into the institution.

His voice was hoarse from all the yelling he did during his preaching. He said "Praise God" between every phrase he uttered, and he spoke carefully and slowly as if to give weight to his every word.

Randy Wayne had grown up with Emmitt and, like most of the town, didn't think much more of him on Jesus than on crack. He was being professional, but his distaste for the man was apparent.

"Randy Wayne," Emmitt said, "how's your relationship with the Lord?"

Randy Wayne cut his widening blue eyes over at me and gave me a wry smile.

"Better than yours, I suspect," he said. "I take his name in vain a lot less than you do."

"If Jesus comes back tonight after turning the moon

to blood, will you be called up to meet him in the clouds or will you be among all the sad, lost souls left behind?"

"Tell you what, after it happens come look for me and see."

"But, brother, I won't be here," Emmitt said sincerely.

"Oh, if there's any truth or justice to any of it you will be."

"I'll pray for you, brother," Emmitt said.

"Please don't," Randy Wayne said.

I had asked Emerson to come early so that he'd enter with one officer on duty in the control room, in this case Randy Wayne, and exit with another. Except it wouldn't be him exiting, it'd be Cardigan in his clothes.

"Who's working tonight?" I asked, trying to make the comment sound offhanded.

"I am," Randy Wayne said. "Fred Moore is sick so I'm pulling a double."

Shit. That means I've got to get Ronnie Cardigan past someone who knows Emmitt very well.

"Sorry. We'll have another volunteer coming in a little before seven."

"No problem."

"These are exciting times, brother," Emmitt said.

We were sitting in my office.

All the inmates were back in the dorms for count. The chapel was empty. The front door was locked. My office door was locked. I had ample time to drug Emmitt, but the more he talked the sooner I wanted to do it.

"To be here when Jesus comes back," he said in his

shout-hoarse voice. "To witness the final blood moon of the tetrad, to see the signs of the End Times. It humbles an ol' sinner like me that Jesus saved me just in time to help usher in his Kingdom."

Yeah, he had been in my office less than five minutes and I couldn't wait another second. Hell, I'd want to drug him even if I didn't have to in order to save Anna.

"I know a lot of people don't think you're saved," he said. "But I think you just need the fire of the Holy Ghost. Have you been baptized in the spirit? Do you speak with other tongues?"

"I want us to pray together," I said.

"Yes, amen," he said. "Praise God."

"But first I want us to take communion together."

"The Lord's Supper. Yes. Hallelujah."

I already had everything set up in the chapel, including his cup with the substance Jake had given me in it.

"Come this way," I said.

I stood and opened the side door that connected my office and the chapel.

He stood and followed.

"I hope you use real wine and bread," he said. "Not wafers and grape juice."

"We're in a prison," I said. "Grape juice is all we're allowed. But even if it weren't, I'm a recovering alcoholic and—"

"You're the one in prison if you believe that," he said. "God can deliver you once and for all. You can be truly set free. Like me. Let me pray for you."

"Let's take communion first," I said. "Kneel here and I'll serve you. Then you can serve me."

He knelt on the carpeted floor between the front pew and the platform. We had no altar or altar table since the interfaith chapel was used for all religions.

I had placed the communion wafers and the plastic chalice filled with grape juice on a tray on the platform beneath a white handkerchief. Removing the small cloth, I lifted the plate of wafers off the tray and turned toward the kneeling Emerson, who was now holding his hands out and up and speaking in tongues.

Forgive me for the sacrilege I'm about to commit.

"The body that was broken for you," I said, holding out the tray to him.

He took a handful of the wafers and tossed them in his mouth like popcorn at a ballgame, then went back to babbling.

The way he took the wafers was a good sign. I needed him to drink enough of the grape juice for it to be effective.

After returning the plate to its place on the platform, I lifted the prison-approved plastic chalice with the grape juice and date rape drug in it—a nonalcoholic version of the cocktail Emmitt was said to have administered to more than one young girl in Pottersville back before Jesus saved him to usher in his Kingdom.

I'm sorry for this.

"The blood that was shed for you," I said, extending the chalice to him.

"The blood of Jesus," he said, taking the cup and sipping from it. "The soul-cleansing blood of the lamb."

He attempted to return the cup to me.

"This one is all yours," I said. "I have another. Take. Drink. Do this in remembrance of me."

He leaned his head back and guzzled the entire cup in a single long gulp, staining the sides of his mouth and chin crimson.

As I turned to replace and re-cover the host, he

began to pray even louder, an angry, aggressive prayer—demanding, disrespectful, egocentric.

I hadn't intended for him to drink the entire cup, but when it looked like he wasn't going to drink enough, I overreacted. I wasn't sure how it worked, how much it took for a man his size, how long it took to go into effect, or how long it would last, but I was fairly certain he had taken a much larger dose than was required.

"Now I'll do you," he said.

"Let's give it a minute to take effect."

"Huh?" he asked, confused. "Brother, the blood of Jesus has an immediate effect. I ass—"

When he tried to stand, he couldn't get his balance and leaned to the right until he fell prostrate on the floor.

"You okay?" I asked.

"Ehhmm feuhhen bruuehuutheuaa."

"I'll take that as a yes."

"Ehmmenn aaissee eeesssuuss."

Chapter Twenty-six

After count cleared and during the chaos of chow, I called down to have Ronnie Cardigan sent to my office.

This not only ensured he'd actually make it to the chapel tonight but would mean he wouldn't be counted as part of the group attending the service.

Since the yard was closed, Cardigan should be escorted to and from the chapel, but in the past when I had called an inmate up while it was still daylight and everyone was busy with the feeding of twenty-five hundred men, I was asked to stand outside the chapel so that the center gate and I could keep an eye on him as he walked up on his own.

And that's exactly what happened.

Center Gate, which was some two hundred yards away, was swarming with inmates, long lines on both sides extending way out on both the upper and lower compounds, as men whose virtually every move was controlled, waited to eat or to return from eating.

Ronnie Cardigan walked alone through the empty upper compound, passing Classification, Medical, Psych, Education, Laundry, and the library, his steps awkward and seemingly self-conscious.

Was it because he knew what we were about to do

and how unlikely it was to work?

"I was planning on attending the service tonight like you asked me to," he said when he reached me. "Is something wrong? Did Mom—"

"Nothing's wrong," I said. "Come on in."

I waved down toward the officer on duty at the center gate, though I doubted he was watching—or could see me even if he were, and we walked into the chapel.

"Did you talk to your family?" I asked.

"I did," he said, his words sounding too loud as they bounced around the hard surfaces of the empty hallway of the chapel.

I paused in the hallway between the door to the darkened library and the staff chaplain's office to talk to Cardigan.

The unconscious and undressed Emmitt Emerson was in my office, and I wanted to go over everything with Cardigan before we went in and exchanged their clothes and prepared to leave.

"What'd they say?" I asked.

"Whatta you mean?"

"About tonight."

"Tonight?" he said, his face wrinkled in confusion. "What about tonight? We just talked about Mom."

"They didn't say anything about tonight?"

"No. Why would they?"

"So you don't know why you're here?" I asked.

He obviously had no idea what was going on, which meant whoever had Anna wasn't his family or hadn't clued him in on the plan.

"What's going on, Chaplain? You're starting to freak me out a little."

"Sorry. I guess there's been some sort of

misunderstanding. Is today your mom's birthday?"

He thought about it. "No. It's not for . . . another two weeks."

It was all I could think of, but I got lucky that it was so close.

"No wonder," I said. "I got the dates confused. I was going to let you call her and wish her a happy birthday."

"That's very nice, Chaplain. But . . . I wonder if she'll still be alive by the time her birthday gets here."

His mom was sick. Very sick if she might not make it to her next birthday. Whoever had Anna knew that much. But did that have anything to do with why they wanted him? Was there another motive? Did his family have anything to do with this?

"Sorry I jumped the gun."

"That's okay. It's a very nice thing to do."

"Come on into the chapel and let's talk for a few minutes."

"Okay."

I led him into the sanctuary where we took a seat on the front pew closest to my side office door.

"What're you in for?" I asked.

He shook his head. "You wouldn't believe me if I told you."

"Try me."

"Bogus drug and burglary charge. I know you hear it all the time. Everybody in here claims to be innocent. I truly am. I've never done a drug in my life. Never sold any drugs. And I've never stolen anything. I'm in the middle of a nightmare like you can't imagine. I keep tryin' to tell people, but . . . no one will listen. Well, nearly no one. Officer Price did. Said he believed me. Said he had a friend who was a TPD cop, would have him look into it, but . . ."

"TPD?"

"Tallahassee. That's where it happened."

"What happened exactly?"

"I'm living my life one moment. Next moment, I'm in here. I was working. Back in school. Doing well. Living in this small, old duplex. Broke as hell, but . . . Then this chick moves into the unit next to mine. She's got guys comin' over all the time. Different guys nearly every day. I figure she's a pro, you know? Like maybe she's working her way through school on her back. I don't like it, don't like having that many strangers around all the time, but . . . none of 'em ever bother me. And she's quiet. A good neighbor. Even when she's entertaining, she's never too loud. Next thing I know, she's dead. Suicide they said. Two days later, I come home from work to find cops searching my place. They find stuff of hers. Jewelry, shit like that. And enough drugs to give me intent to distribute. None of it mine. Girl was pregnant. They did a DNA test. Proved the baby wasn't mine, but didn't help my case none."

"Any of the investigators indicate it might not have been suicide?"

He nodded. "They were looking at me for killin' her. Said they'd've pressed it if the kid had been mine. Said I was lucky to just be going down for stealing her shit."

"That's what they said?" I asked. "I mean that's the way they said it?"

"Yeah, why?"

"Like the drugs were hers too. They thought you stole them from her."

"Guess so. No one ever said that exactly, but . . . . I guess that could be what they meant."

"Did you ever actually see or hear her having sex with the parade of guys? Was it just guys or girls too?"

"Sometimes. Yeah, some girls. Why?"

"Just thinkin' maybe she was a dealer and not a prostitute," I said. "Or maybe both. Did Officer Price find out anything?"

He shrugged. "Said he'd let me know, but . . ."

"You know his first name or initial?"

He shook his head.

"What dorm does he work in?"

"Was in B Dorm. Don't know where he is now."

"What made you tell him?"

"Told any and everyone who'd listen. He's the only one said he'd do anything."

Chapter Twenty-seven

"**I**'ll look into your case," I said.

"*You?*"

I nodded. "Used to be a cop. Still an investigator."

"Really? Wow. Okay. Thanks," he said as if grateful but doubtful.

"In the meantime, how would you like to see your mother?"

I had to figure out a way to talk him into leaving the institution with me tonight.

"I told you. I'd *love* to see her."

"You also told me you'd do anything to get to," I said.

"Well . . ."

"You feel differently now? You said you'd be willing to get more time if you could see her."

"No, I mean, I would, but . . ."

"But what?"

"I think maybe I got a ticket out of here."

"Oh yeah? What's that?"

"Don't want to say. Just something I think I can leverage. We'll see."

"But what if I told you you could see your mom now, tonight?"

"How?"

"I'd help you."

"How?"

"Do you want to or not?"

"Do you mean a furlough or . . . something else?"

"Something else. Getting out, but risking more time when you turn yourself back in."

He grew very still and quiet and seemed to consider what I had said with great intensity.

I hadn't foreseen this, couldn't have predicted his hesitation—not based on what he had told me earlier.

Finally, he shook his head. "I . . . think I'll wait to see if what I have goin' can . . . do the same thing but without adding time to my sentence."

How can I get him out now?

I looked longingly toward the empty chalice peeking out of the small white cloth from the edge of the platform, and felt like Juliet must have felt.

"You won't get any additional time," I said. "You won't serve another day. We'll get the case against you dismissed. I'll make sure of it. You're really innocent, right?"

He was nodding vigorously before I finished. "I am. I really am. I swear it."

"So?"

He shrugged. "I don't know . . . What if you can't?"

"I feel pretty certain I can. I'm pretty good at this. But what do you have to lose?"

"More of my life."

"A *little* more, maybe, for the chance to see your mom before she . . . before it's too late. Think about it."

I can't believe I'm having to hard sell this.

"Why do you want me to so bad? Why do you even

care?"

Think fast.

"Lots of reasons. I told your family I would. My mom just died and I miss her far more than I ever thought was possible. I've looked at your case and believe you're innocent."

"My family asked you to?"

"It's why I asked if you had spoken to them."

"They didn't say anything."

"The calls are monitored. They can't say anything to you about it."

"Then why'd you want me to talk to them?"

"Thought they might say something to you in code. Something only you'd understand."

"Wait. They did. Dad did. I didn't . . . know what . . . he meant at the time, but . . . Okay. Let's do this. How do we?"

I told him.

"Really?" he said. "That's it? I don't know. You really think that'll work?"

"I do."

I have to.

"Okay."

The front door to the chapel opened and inmates started filing into the hallway. Talking Ronnie into this had taken far longer than I thought it would.

"Come on," I said. "Let's go into my office and get you changed."

I grabbed the communion tray and we quickly ducked into my office.

"Have a seat," I said, nodding toward one of the chairs across from my desk. "Let me check in with them. I'll be right back."

He nodded. "Okay."

I opened my other office door and stepped into the front hallway.

Inmates pouring through the double doors of the chapel, through the hallway, into the double doors to the sanctuary where Cardigan and I had just been. An officer near the door, his radio squawking. The volunteer shaking my hand and saying hi as he went by.

I waved to the officer and went back into my office.

"I thought you said there was someone here I was swapping places with?" Cardigan asked when I sat down behind my desk across from him.

"There is."

"Where is he?"

I nodded to the small door in the back corner behind him. "Bathroom."

Eventually, all the inmates finished filing into the sanctuary and the volunteer began his study, the officer, as usual, observing from the back corner.

"Okay," I said. "Let's get you changed. Take a minute and take some deep breaths, settle and prepare yourself. I'll get your clothes."

He nodded.

I stepped over to the small restroom, opened the door just wide enough for me to squeeze through, and closed it behind me.

The small, tiled room was the size of a tiny closet, with only a lidless, tankless toilet and a sink.

Emmitt Emerson was slumped on the toilet in his underwear, unconscious. Confirming again he still had a pulse, I grabbed his clothes and shoes and went back into my office, closing the narrow door behind me.

"Come over here behind my desk and change," I said.

There was a narrow strip of glass on the door to my

office, but the back corner of my desk was partially blocked
by the small wall of the sanctuary sound booth.

He did.

"Put on everything," I said. "T-shirt. Socks. Shoes.
Tie. Leave everything in the pockets."

"Can't believe I'm doing this," he said.

Me either.

"What do I do with these?" he asked, holding up his
inmate uniform and brogans.

"I'll take them." Which I did, and placed them in the
bathroom with Emmitt.

"How do I look?"

"A lot like Emmitt Emerson."

"Who?"

"The guy whose clothes you're borrowing."

"That's good, right?"

I nodded. "That's great."

A knock at the door and we both jumped.

I turned to see the officer who was supposed to
be keeping an eye on the inmates in the chapel looking
through the narrow window of my door.

"Chaplain, can I use your phone for a minute?"

He wanted to make a personal call. Anything
institutional and he could've used his radio.

I walked over and opened the door only wide
enough for my head, which I poked out and in a whisper
said, "Someone's using it right now."

"Oh. Sorry."

He started to head back toward the chapel, but
stopped, turned, and said, "Who's here? Thought it was just
us."

Us must have meant me, him, the volunteer leading
the service, and the hundred or so inmates.

"Another volunteer. Emmitt Emerson."

"I didn't know I had to supervise another service tonight."

"You don't. It got canceled. He's very sick. I'm about to help him get home."

He nodded. "I'll walk up to control and get a key for your office so I can use the phone when you leave."

If he also used the private restroom, which was likely, he'd see the real Emmitt doing his Elvis impersonation on the toilet.

"That's too long to be away from your post," I said. "Come with me. You can use the phone in the staff chaplain's office. Just be quick."

I led him down the hallway and unlocked the staff chaplain's office for him.

"Hurry. I'll watch the inmates until you get back."

"They're fine. It's okay."

"Words spoken right before every riot, assault, murder, or escape," I said. "I'm locking the offices before I leave and I'm leaving in five minutes. Make it quick and get back to your post."

"I don't take orders from preachers."

"Not a problem," I said. "I'll get the captain to tell you."

"Fuck man. Just forget it. Jesus."

He slowly walked past me, mad muggin' all the way.

"Just wanted to use the fuckin' phone for five minutes. Shit."

I closed the door behind him and went back over to my office. Before I went in, I said, "I'll be back in a little while, but I'm gonna have the OIC drop in and check on things while I'm gone."

Chapter Twenty-eight

"You ready?" I asked

"Not really," Cardigan said.

Me either, but . . .

I had just walked back into my office and for a fraction of a second thought I was looking at Emmitt Emerson.

"What happens if I'm recognized or they don't buy that I'm what's-his-name Emerson?" Cardigan said.

"I'll take care of it," I said. "I'll take care of everything. Just go with what I do. You're so sick you can hardly stand up. You certainly can't talk."

"Okay."

"As we go, lean on me. Let me help you walk. Keep your head down like you're about to throw up."

"I probably will be."

We walked out of the cool chapel into the warm, darkening night and headed toward the front gate.

Pulse elevated, mind racing.

The pale moon above us was big and bright and only partially shadowed so far, its shrinking circumference shimmering in a kind of translucent duskiness.

I half held Cardigan up as we hobbled toward the first of the two gates we had to get through, him with one arm around me and his head hanging down.

"Don't overdo it," I said. "You're sick, not incapacitated."

If he was too convincing, the control room would send help and maybe even call an ambulance.

He straightened a bit and we moved a little faster toward our fate.

The moon looked like a charcoal drawing sketched in the shimmering sky, streaks and smudges of darkness around the edges, shadings and highlights, powder and pencil dusting the surface.

When we reached the first gate of the pedestrian sally port, I placed my fingers through the chain-link and pulled, rattling the gate a bit—usually all that was required to alert the control room to my presence and be buzzed through.

But nothing happened.

I waited, my heart pounding now, and tried to breathe deeply and calmly.

"What's wrong?" Cardigan whispered, fear at the ragged edges of his voice.

Tower One loomed above us in the blackening night sky, the armed officer on duty authorized to fire if he suspected what we were doing.

I lowered my head a bit and looked back down the compound.

All was quiet and dark, no officers or response team running toward us.

I rattled the gate again.

And waited.

"Let's go back to the chapel," Cardigan said. "Come on. Before it's too late."

And waited some more.

"Just a little longer," I said. "Maybe they haven't—"

"Chaplain," someone yelled from behind me.

"*Oh fuck*," Cardigan said. "*Fuck*."

I turned to see an officer I recognized but couldn't name jogging toward us.

Until this moment I had thought about what I might do if I couldn't get Cardigan out of the institution, but not about what would happen if I got caught trying to get him out and was unable to go to meet the kidnappers at all.

If we're caught, Anna is dead.

Think. What do I do?

"Chaplain," the officer said again. "What is it? Everything okay?"

"Sick volunteer," I said. "Helping him home. Can't get anyone in the control room to open the gate for us."

"I'll radio Sergeant Davis," he said. "Must be dealing with an incident or on the phone."

"Thank you."

"Chaplain's at the interior gate, Serg," he said into his radio. "Got a sick volunteer we need to get out of here."

The lock on the gate popped and we walked in, the officer closing it behind us.

"Thanks again," I said to him. "I really appreciate your help."

"No problem," he said, and headed back over toward the visiting park.

We moved over to the control room window, Cardigan leaning on me, head down.

I unclipped my ID badge and held it up to the window, placing it in the small adhesive frame put there for that reason.

Randy Wayne didn't even look at it, just waved me through.

"Almost there," I said to Cardigan. "Hang on. Hold it together."

The electronic lock popped on the outside gate and it eased open a few inches. I stepped toward it, shoved it open, helped Cardigan through it, and slammed it shut behind us.

We had taken a few steps away, walking toward the admin building and the parking lot beyond, when Randy Wayne opened the document tray and yelled for me.

I slowed and turned back, but kept moving away.

He leaned down and yelled out the window, "You need help?"

"Nah. I'm just gonna drive him home. I'll be back in a few. Thanks."

"Everything okay in the chapel? I need to send someone down to help out?"

"It's all good. I'll be back by the end of the service to lock up and—"

"Hey, Emmitt," he yelled. "I thought blood-bought, saved, sanctified, filled-with-the-Holy Ghost faith-healer evangelists didn't get sick. Especially during a blood moon when the world is ending."

I smiled and waved to him and continued walking.

Chapter Twenty-nine

Night.

Woods.

Path.

Damp dirt. Warm air. Stillness.

Quietude.

The umbra of earth's shadow crawled across the moon, darkness spreading like black fog over the pale white surface.

The quiet night had a hushed quality about it, as if the aura of the lunar event was casting something ethereal on the earth, the ephemeral nature of which caused a certain celestial reverence.

I had driven around the long way and parked at Potter Farm.

On the drive, I had taken the small snub-nosed .38 from beneath my seat and slipped it into my pocket.

As expected, Potter Farm was empty, no light or movement in the farmhouse or barn.

We were now traversing the small path that led down to the pond and to the deeper woods beyond, and beyond those to a field beyond which was the prison complex.

The trail was narrow and overgrown, bushes and branches sharp and pointy and thorned, hanging, leaning, looming.

Flashes of a figure in a party dress running, stumbling, tripping, falling down this very path. Not long ago.

Cuts. Scrapes. Abrasions.

Another figure. Chasing. Former friend. Now killer.

Broken heels. Sprained ankle. Adrenaline-juiced heart ricocheting around ribcage.

Anna and I had walked this path before. Down to the pond on our lunch break. Enjoying each other in a seclusion that felt Edenic.

Was she somewhere on this path now?

Would we be together soon?

Or would this path that had once been for us a secret garden become our own personal Via Dolorosa, the way of suffering and blood?

"Where are we meeting them?" Ronnie asked.

"Not sure. Just somewhere along the path. Us walking it gives them a chance to ensure we're alone."

"Hope it's not too much longer," he said. "Dude's shoes don't fit my feet."

Though strictly speaking not my hostage, I had him walking in front of me, far enough so he couldn't spin around and attack me without me seeing it coming.

I had to at least consider that he could be feigning ignorance and actually be a part of a plan that included bashing my head in.

We reached a spot on the path where the moon could be seen without obstruction. We both paused and looked up.

Darkness had spread across the face of the moon, its slow expansion toward eclipse reaching beyond the halfway mark.

"How much longer 'til it's eclipsed?" Ronnie asked.

"Not sure. Takes a while. It's something to see."

He nodded. "Really is. Cool how it changes everything about the night."

He was right. The normally noisy woods were as quiet as I had ever heard them, the usual nocturnal chatter, the hums and saws and buzzes and chirps, nonexistent.

After another moment, we continued on.

Was this a setup? Would we be ambushed? Had I played this all wrong? Was Anna already dead?

I wondered if we were being watched—perhaps through a night vision scope or infrared goggles. Dying was one thing. Failing to save Anna was another.

I could feel the tension in my neck and shoulders, the pounding of my pulse in my throat and head, and though it was warm, I was sweating far more profusely than if just from the heat.

"Something's not right," Cardigan said. "Feels off. You feel it?"

"It's just the moon," I said. "And nerves."

"I don't know. Seems like more than that. Feels like I'm gonna die tonight."

"You're not. It's gonna be okay. It'll all be over soon."

"Over?"

"I just meant . . . you'll be with your mom. Hold it together just a little longer."

As we walked, I scanned the woods, searching the darkness for darker figures, letting my eyes wander both sides of the path for movement.

Every few steps, I paused, listened, checked behind me.

There was no one. Anywhere.

Just because you don't see them doesn't mean they're not there.

I realize that, but . . .

We seemed to be alone.

Eventually, we reached the small pond the path had been sloping toward. Though rimmed by cypress trees and pond pines, an opening across the way made the moon visible.

Earth's umbra was nearly three-quarters across the diminishing orb.

Seen in the reflection on the smooth surface of the pond below, the shimmering, shadowed moon appeared even more mystical as it moved atop the gently undulating waters.

"Nobody here," he said. "What's really going on? Is this all some sort of—

"Just be patient a few more minutes," I said. "I still think they'll show. They're probably just being cautious. That's a good thing."

"They—whoever *they* are—are probably about to cap us. No warning. No time to . . . we'll just be here one moment and gone the next. Never know what hit us."

I'm having a hard time not hitting you.

We stepped off the path and made our way down to the pond, standing at the dark water's edge like two naïve supplicants awed in the face of an inexplicable phenomenon.

"See anything?" Ronnie asked.

I shook my head—something he couldn't see in my position beside and just behind him. "Nothing yet. I'll tell you when I—"

"John? Is that you?"

The disembodied voice was the same one from the phone, the one that haunted me, the one that echoed through my dreams, the one I'd never forget no matter how long I lived.

"I'm here," I said.

Not only could I not see anyone, I had a difficult time distinguishing where the voice was coming from.

"Who's with you?"

"Who you asked me to bring," I said. "Ronnie Cardigan."

"Who are you?" Ronnie yelled, surprised. "Whatta you want with me?"

"John, stay where you are. Send Cardigan around the pond to your right to meet me and I'll send Anna around to the left to you."

"Okay."

I searched for any movement, any sign of Anna.

To my left, through the trees and undergrowth, light from the prison backlit an area of mostly pines and I could see Anna beginning to ease her way through them.

"I ain't goin' until you tell me who you are and what you want me for," Ronnie yelled.

"Thought the chaplain would've told you. To see your mom. Your family hired me to get you out and bring you to her."

"Who?"

"Who what?" the kidnapper asked. "You need to walk this way—to your right. John you need to send him over here now. We'll grab Anna again if you don't. Anna stop where you are. Don't move until Ronnie starts heading over here."

Anna continued walking.

"Who hired you?" Cardigan said.

"Anna stop where you are or we'll shoot."

"I did what you asked me to," I said. "Leave her alone. Let her keep coming."

"Something's not right," Ronnie said to me.

"I told you," the kidnapper said. Your family."

I watched Anna as she continued toward me, tracking her progress. Things were unraveling. If the balloon went up, I wanted to be able to get to her fast.

"No. Who in my family?" Cardigan said. "I don't buy it, don't believe you."

"Your dad. Who else?"

"My dad's been dead for three years," Ronnie yelled. "Oh shit."

Ronnie looked over at me. "You just got me killed," he said. "My dad's not dead, but they don't know it. What's really going on here?"

"Grab him," the kidnapper yelled.

A rustling in the underbrush, fast footfalls, running, snapping branches, crunching twigs.

"Follow me if you want to live," I said.

"GET HIM NOW."

I took off running toward Anna, the .38 out now, in my right hand. At my side. Pointed toward the ground. Hammer back. Finger on the trigger.

"Stay with me," I said. "I'll protect you."

"Fuck that," he said, and took off in the opposite direction.

Running.

Stumbling over tree limbs. Slipping on pine straw. Twisting around tree trunks. Bushes and plants and branches impeding my progress.

Looking for Anna. Scanning. Searching.

Shots fired. Small caliber gun. *Pop. Pop.*

"ANNA," I yelled. "GET DOWN. STAY DOWN. I'LL FIND YOU."

"WE WON'T HURT HER, JOHN," the kidnapper yelled. "SHE'S SAFE. YOU BOTH ARE. YOU DID WHAT WE—"

Another shot. *Pop.* Then another. *Pop.*

"STOP SHOOTING FOR FUCK'S SAKE."

Still running.

Dress shoes sinking in soggy sand, sliding down the small embankment toward the pond.

"Anna," I said.

"John."

She was there. Not far away now. So close.

Get to her.

Diving beside her, I grabbed her. Hugged her. Held her.

She felt so good.

"You okay?"

"Am now."

"JOHN," Merrill yelled from the other side of the pond. "ONE RUNNING YOUR WAY."

I was shocked to hear Merrill's voice, but didn't think about it, just responded to what he said.

Spinning around in a crouch, I came up behind Anna, shielding her body with mine, gun up, eyes scanning the area behind the barrel.

In the glow of the institution, I could see a figure sprinting—but away from and not toward us, perpendicular to the prison.

Then more rustling and running from the opposite side.

A shout I couldn't make out. Another shot. Different gun this time.

A figure running toward us. Cardigan. Getting close. Merrill behind him, gaining.

Urge to stand, move toward him. Staying with Anna.

Merrill overtaking him, tripping him. Cardigan crashing hard on the forest floor.

Merrill snatching him up, zip-tying his wrists behind

him, moving over toward us.

"Think they only two of 'em," he said. "One down. One runnin'."

"What're you doin' here?" I asked.

Chapter Thirty

"Her ex," Merrill said.

"Huh?"

I was helping Anna to her feet, continuing to scan the area as I did.

"Are you okay?" I asked her.

She nodded.

I hugged and kissed her and held her for a long moment.

Above us, the moon continued to disappear incrementally.

"Whatta you mean, my ex?" Anna asked.

"He hobblin' over here," Merrill said, jerking his head back in the direction he had just come from. "I'a let him tell you."

"*He's alive?*" Anna asked.

"But we better walk toward him if we want to see him anytime soon."

We did.

As we made our way over toward Chris Taunton, who was moving like a man who should be in the hospital, I checked behind us periodically.

"Not her ex," Chris said when we got near him. "Not yet."

"Tell 'em how your ass helped save the day and my ass," Merrill said.

He looked at me. "Day I checked myself out of the hospital and came to your house to ask you again if I could help you," he said. "When you left, I went inside and looked around. Found the letter you left for Merrill."

"Brought it to me and asked what we should do," Merrill said. "We been watchin' you ever since."

"I didn't want to do anything to risk Anna's life," Chris said. "But I didn't want to not do anything that might help save her."

"Thank you," she said.

Chris had turned and started his way back toward the path. We had all matched his pace, moving slowly out of the bowl that formed the lake, up toward the trail we had walked in on, Merrill with a hand on the cuffed Cardigan.

"It's not just my wife but my child we're talkin' about," he said.

"So we watch and wait," Merrill said. "Follow you out here tonight and—"

Ronnie said, "I didn't do anything wrong. Why am I cuffed?"

"You ran," I said. "In the wrong direction."

"Then your ass ran from me," Merrill said.

"I didn't know what was going on. Guys in correctional uniforms. Guns goin' off. Figured y'all brought me out here to kill me 'cause of what I know."

"Which is what?" Merrill said.

"How I know you not in on it?" he said. "Ain't sayin' shit."

My arm was around Anna. I held her as we walked. I had no intention of ever letting go again.

"What happened?" I asked. "Why would they let

Anna go and then start shooting before Ronnie even made it over there? And where is the other guy, the one who didn't run?"

"Soon as they let Anna go and start shootin'," Merrill said, "I start easin' up on 'em. Then this fool"— nodding toward Cardigan—"come running up behind me and knock me down. I look up and they got the drop on me. My ass staring up at the barrel of a cannon."

"A cannon?" I said.

"Well, least a .357. Do this fool help? No, he off runnin' again—in the opposite direction this time."

I continued to glance behind us, making sure there weren't more of them or that the one who ran hadn't doubled back to come up behind us.

"What was I supposed to do?" Cardigan said.

"Hop-along Taunton here with a little hitch in his giddy-up stumble out of the bushes and shoots the guy. Save my black ass from dyin' in the dirt where I sat."

"He's dead?" Anna said.

"As I would've been," Merrill said.

"Thank you," I said to Chris.

"Yes, thank you," Anna said.

"For everything," I said.

Chris shrugged. "Happened so fast I didn't have time to think. If I had . . ."

When we reached the path, the last of the moon's paleness appeared to be vanishing, as if evanescent in nature—a vapor instead of a planet.

Merrill looked at his watch. "Whatcha say you don't do any jail time," he said to me. "Maybe even save your job. You might just have time to get him back in before anybody realize he gone. Call your dad on the way. Tell him what's what. We stay and wait for him."

"Could work," I said.

"Worth a shot," he said.

"And tell him to send an ambulance," Chris said. "I think I ripped something open."

"Okay," I said. "Wish me luck."

"I'm going with you," Anna said.

I nodded.

"I mean everywhere. For the rest of my life."

Chapter Thirty-one

"You sure you didn't recognize him?" I asked.

Anna, Cardigan, and I were in her Mustang racing back toward the institution. I was driving, Anna was in the seat beside me, Cardigan stuffed in the nearly nonexistent backseat.

Anna had been telling me every detail she could recall from her time with the kidnappers while they were fresh on her mind, and my question to Cardigan had been intentionally abrupt.

Before we had left the path near the pond, we had taken Ronnie over to look at the kidnapper to see if we could get an ID on him, which was the reason for my question now as I looked at him in the rearview mirror.

"Positive," Cardigan said. "Never seen him before in my life."

The kidnapper was just that. A kid. His youthful appearance matched the voice I had been hearing on the phone.

He was a pale, blond-haired, blue-eyed boy in his early twenties, in khaki pants and a light blue short-sleeved sport shirt. Average height. Average build. Though not overweight, there was a certain softness about his body. He looked more like a camp counselor or fast food manager than a kidnapper.

His soft body was sprawled out across the narrow path, his pale-blue shirt wet with blood, blood that looked black in what was left of the moonlight.

"He was so young," Anna said.

"Wonder who he is and what he wanted with me?" Cardigan said.

"Dad will try to get an ID first thing."

"He was genuinely good to me," Anna said. "Incredibly so. It's not Stockholm syndrome. He really was."

I looked in the rearview mirror at Cardigan again. "You said you wondered what he wanted with you," I said, "but you probably know."

"I'm not lying. I really don't."

"Think about it," I said. "Only a couple of things it can be."

"Well, please enlighten me," he said, "'cause I honestly don't know."

"Could be what he said. Your family. And it just went wrong. But if it's not, there are two obvious possibilities I can see, and I just met you."

"Let's hear them."

"Your case. You claim to be innocent."

"I am."

"If that's true, it could be whoever's guilty. Or maybe someone who believes you're guilty of not only robbing your neighbor but killing her too."

"Hadn't thought of that. What's the other?"

"You know what it is. You keep talkin' about knowing something that's going to help you get out. Hasn't crossed your mind it could be connected to that? Wanna tell me what you know?" I said. "I can't help you if I don't know what it is."

"You should let him help you," Anna said.

"I don't know that you're not involved. I don't know you. I could've gotten killed tonight."

"It doesn't have to be one of those," I said. "It could be one of a thousand different things I know nothing about. Those two are just obvious from what I know about you and what you've told me about your case."

He didn't say anything.

"I'm willing to look into your case," I said, "see if I can help you. But I can't do it if I lose my job and go to jail."

"I don't understand," he said.

Anna squeezed my hand. "You risked so much for me."

"Are you gonna work with me to get you back into the institution, in your uniform, and back into your dorm? Not gonna say anything? Not gonna sabotage what I'm about to try?"

"I won't. Helping you helps me. I don't want to be out here like this. I don't want to do anything to risk spending even one second more than I have to in there."

"I hope you'll remember that," I said.

"Whatta we gonna do?" Anna asked.

"See if we can get him back in before the service is over in the chapel. Get him changed and back in the dorm. Then get Emmitt Emerson out."

"You should tell us what you know," Anna said. "Let us help you. We owe you."

"You already know," he said. "If you think about it. It's all anybody's talking about."

We didn't say anything. I didn't know what he was referring to.

"A certain . . . investigation going on right now."

"Into the death of Hahn Ling?" I asked.

"No. It involves a group of officers."

There were always investigations involving correctional officers, but there was only one he could be talking about.

Three correctional officers were under investigation for a use-of-force incident that led to the death of inmate Reggie Dalton.

If found guilty, Officers Marty Perkins, Lewis Milner, and Sergeant Jack Kirkus would be fired and arrested on charges of official misconduct and manslaughter or murder.

The incident involving twenty-eight-year-old Reggie Dalton, who was serving a twenty-year sentence for drug trafficking and armed robbery, was being investigated by Rachel Peterson and her office, with additional assistance from FDLE.

There were a lot of questions surrounding the case, but video footage from both the use-of-force camcorder and the prison surveillance system seemed to exonerate the officers and demonstrate they did nothing excessive. However, one crucial video feed from the surveillance system was missing and the camcorder recording appeared to have been stopped and restarted, leading to questions of whether the equipment involved had malfunctioned or been disabled.

The footage showed Dalton being belligerent, yelling obscenities, refusing orders, antagonizing the officers, and eventually slinging feces from his cell. A chemical agent was used to subdue the inmate, and on the way to the decontamination shower, he somehow broke free and assaulted the officers. He was eventually subdued again, but shortly after collapsed and was taken to the hospital. He died en route.

"The Reggie Dalton case?" I asked.

"Ain't sayin' anything else. Said too much already."

My phone vibrated in my pocket.

It was Merrill.

"Hey."

"Your dad, some deputies, and one of his investigators just arrived. Ambulance takin' Taunton back to the hospital. They gonna interview him there. Me, here or the sheriff's department. While I was waitin' on 'em to get here, I might have searched the kid's pockets for ID, and between his wallet, business card, and his website, which I might have glanced at on my phone, discovered a few things."

"Like what?" I said. "Hypothetically."

"Like his name is Karl Jason. Like he live in Tallahassee. Like he a thespian and not a thug. He a theater adjunct at TCC and audition a lot. Does a lot of theater. Been in a few local commercials and student films. Had a small role in Victor Nunez's last joint."

"Thanks man."

"Just 'cause he a actor don't mean he was actin'."

"True."

"But it probably do. He most likely hired to play a part."

"Most likely," I said. "And that would explain some things."

"And call some others into question."

Chapter Thirty-two

"How are you feeling?" I asked Anna.

We were still holding hands, still driving toward the institution.

"I'm okay," she said. "Really. I need a shower in the worst kind of way, and I'm tired—haven't slept well without you. I'm emotional, of course. It's been an ordeal, but . . . I'm okay."

"I'm so . . ." I started, but got choked up. "I'm so happy to have you back."

"I missed you so much," she said. "Part of me thought I'd never see you again. I thought . . . there's no way they'll just let me go. But . . . I knew if anybody could save me . . ."

We fell silent a moment, something beyond words passing between us.

The night grew darker, but only the night.

Before us, the moon looked like a petri dish with black mold overtaking it. Beneath it, the prison glowed more brightly in the darkness.

"We're almost there," I said to Cardigan in the rearview mirror. "Sure you don't want to tell me more?"

"Yeah, I'm good."

"The name Karl Jason mean anything to you?"

"No. Why? Should it?"

The three of us walked toward the control room. Slowly. Deliberately.

When we got close I veered off and went over to talk to Randy Wayne Davis through the document tray while Anna and Cardigan walked straight to the gate and waited for me.

Randy Wayne looked at me with wide eyes, a quizzical expression on the tired face beneath his raised eyebrows.

"He got to feeling better," I said.

He shook his head and frowned. "It's a miracle."

"He left his Bible and notes in the chapel," I said. "I'm gonna take him in to get them and check on everything."

"And Anna?" he asked. "She feeling better?"

"She is. Thanks. She needs to grab a few things out of her office too."

"Oh hell," she said on cue. "I forgot my keys. Can you grab me a set?"

"She forgot her keys," I said. "Can I get a set for her?"

He looked suspicious and a little annoyed, but he located the keys, logged them out to me, then popped the lock on the gate for us.

We walked through both gates and toward the chapel, something I honestly believed I'd never do again.

Unlocking the front door to the chapel, I stepped aside and let Anna and Ronnie walk in first.

The service was still going strong in the sanctuary.

The officer watching from the back turned to look at us, but when I waved he looked away.

We went into my office and they sat down while I stepped into the bathroom and checked on Emmitt.

He was still out, but seemed to be rousing a bit, mumbling and moving a little.

I grabbed Ronnie's inmate uniform from the floor and closed the door behind me.

"Change behind my desk again," I said, placing the pile of clothes in my chair and stepping out of the way. "Quickly as you can."

Without wasting any time, he hopped up, went around behind my desk, and began to change—seemingly unselfconscious in front of Anna.

"What now?" Anna asked.

I moved over to her and began rubbing her shoulders.

She added, "I got my keys in case you wanted me to look up anything or pull any files."

"I know you don't feel like any of that," I said. "We'll get Cardigan safely back to his dorm and wait until Emerson's wife can come get him, then we'll get you home—into a warm shower and soft bed."

"I'm good. Really. Happy to help. I have a change of clothes in my desk. I'll clean up and wash my hair in the sink and I'll feel good as new."

"But—"

"I know you want to work it, try to figure out what's going on. I'll help you. If I get too tired or to feeling bad, I'll let you know and we can go home. I promise. I really am fine."

"You sure?"

"Positive. I want to know too. Too keyed up to sleep."

"You're perfect," I said.

"Perfect for you."

"Okay," Ronnie said, placing Emmitt's clothes and shoes on my desk. "I'm done."

I picked up Emmitt's pants and began to go through the pockets.

"You think I took something?" Ronnie asked, his voice equal parts hurt and indignation.

"Not doing my job if I don't make sure."

"What the hell is *your job*, exactly?" he asked.

I opened the wallet. Emmitt's debit card was missing. When I looked up Ronnie was holding it out to me. "Had to try. Sorry."

I continued searching. The toothpick was missing too.

This time when I looked up, he was holding out a five dollar bill.

"Hadn't gotten to that yet," I said. "I was at the toothpick."

"What if that's the only thing that keeps me alive?"

I held out my hand. "Why not just give me everything? Save some time."

He handed me the five, the toothpick, a nickel, and a picture of Emmitt's wife, a pale Pentecostal woman with no makeup, bad skin, and unfortunate features.

"Really?" I said.

"Beggars can't be choosers. You ever heard that?"

As I was returning the items to Emmitt's wallet and the wallet to his pants, the phone on my desk rang.

I slid past Ronnie to pick it up.

He walked around and sat in the empty seat across my desk beside Anna.

"Chaplain Jordan."

"Chaplain, it's Randy Wayne. I just got a call from

B Dorm. Did you call an inmate Cardigan up earlier this evening? They can't locate him now."

"I did and he's still here. We're wrapping up now if you want to send someone for him."

"But you left the institution," he said. "How—"

"He sat in the service while I was away."

"Oh. Okay. Are you sure everything's okay? You're acting odd tonight."

"Just tired. Thank you. I was just about to walk Ms. Rodden down to her office. You want me to escort Cardigan to the center gate?"

"Thanks. I'll have someone waiting for him."

I placed Emmitt's clothes in the bathroom with him, and Ronnie, Anna, and I were on the move again.

The night we stepped out into was different than the one we had been in earlier.

Darkness covered the face of the moon and shrouded the earth. The eclipse nearly complete, the moon was now beginning to turn red, its circumference rimmed with it, its face blushing crimson.

When we reached Classification, I hugged Anna and kissed her. "Lock yourself in. I'll call you when I get back to my office. When you finish, call me and I'll come get you."

"Love you," she said.

After she was inside and the door locked behind her, I walked Ronnie the rest of the way.

"I'll check on you in the morning," I said. "If you need anything or change your mind about telling me what you know, have your dorm officer get in touch with me."

He nodded. "Okay."

"Thanks for your help tonight," I said. "I won't forget it."

"Just get me out of here and we'll call it even."

Chapter Thirty-three

Back in my office, I called Anna at her desk.

"I'm fine. I'm gonna clean up, change, then see what I can find out about Cardigan's case. I'll call you when I have something. Let me know what else you need me to do. And go ahead and dress Emerson. I don't want to be there for that."

Which was what I was doing when Dad called.

"Merrill filled me in," he said.

"Thanks for trusting and helping me," I said.

"Is Anna okay?"

"She is."

"Told you Chris's gunshot wound wasn't self-inflicted," he said.

"But you suspected me of doing it."

He laughed. "Can't get 'em all right."

We were quiet a moment, Emmitt beginning to moan a little in the background.

"How'd you do it?" he asked.

"What?"

"Get the inmate out. Were you able to get him back in without anyone knowing?"

"Yeah, he's in. Can I tell you how I got him out a little later? Still trying to wrap things up here."

"You bet. We're interviewing Merrill and Chris, but it's a clean shoot. Self-defense. Glad they were here. Wish it could've been me. Soon as I have a positive ID or any info on the shooter, I'll let you know. Name's Karl Jason according to his driver's license. From Tallahassee. We're searching for the one who ran. Got a few roadblocks set up, but nothing so far."

When we hung up, I returned to dressing Emmitt, a challenge in the small, narrow restroom.

As I did, I thought more about the kidnappers' motive and how everything went down. If it really did have something to do with what Cardigan saw or knew about the Reggie Dalton case, then the threat was inside the prison and Ronnie was still in danger.

I stopped dressing Emmitt again, stepped over to my desk, and called the control room.

"What can I do you for, Chaplain?" Randy Wayne asked.

"Can you have the OIC call me?"

"He's up here now," he said. "Hold on a minute and I'll feed the phone through to him."

"Captain Lloyd."

"Captain, it's Chaplain Jordan. I've been counseling with an inmate tonight, Ronnie Cardigan from B Dorm, and I'm worried about him. Can you have him watched overnight until I can meet with him again in the morning?"

"We talkin' SOS cell, PM, or Confinement?"

"He's not suicidal. I'm just concerned about him. He may be in some danger from somebody in the institution— another inmate or even a staff member. I'm not sure. I just want to make sure he's protected until I can figure out more."

"You got it. I'll call down and have it done now."

"Thank you."

"Y'all 'bout to wrap up the services in the chapel?"

"Yes. Just a little longer."

When we hung up, I called the control room right back. It was busy.

I waited for a few moments, then called again.

"Forget something?" Randy Wayne asked.

"Need an outside line," I said.

"Number?"

I withdrew Rachel Peterson's card from my wallet and gave him her cell so he could log it. As soon as I did, I could hear a dial tone. I punched in her number.

"Rachel Peterson."

"It's John Jordan. Is an inmate named Ronnie Cardigan one of your witnesses in the Reggie Dalton case?"

"You know I can't tell you that."

"I think he's in danger. Just wanted to see if you were keeping an eye on him."

"Oh. Well, he's not one of mine, so . . ."

"Okay. Thanks. Sorry I disturbed you. 'Night."

Maybe I was wrong about which case Cardigan had been referring to or maybe he was involved and she wasn't aware of it. Of course, maybe what was going on had nothing to do with what he thinks he knows. It could have to do with his original case or something else entirely.

I turned and looked at the unconscious, partially dressed Emmitt, who was still slumped on the toilet.

"There's no way to know without more info," I said to him. "You know?"

He didn't respond.

"If you disagree you can tell me," I said.

The door to the sanctuary opened and inmates began lining up in the hallway outside my office.

I stepped over and closed the restroom door, then went out into the hallway and thanked the volunteer and greeted the inmates, several of whom launched into complaints, requests, and grievances.

Though I thanked the officer, he continued to ignore me.

He ordered the inmates to line up outside the chapel, and I walked the volunteer out into the black, blood-tinged night.

We both stopped and looked up, beholding the brilliant blood moon as if with a catch in our throats.

"Looks like a darker, more glowing version of Mars," he said.

And it did.

I stood and waited as he made his way to the front gate and the inmates began their much longer journey to the center gate and their housing beyond, all the while staring up at the blood-red orb shimmering in the black night sky.

Chapter Thirty-four

Back inside my office, I finished dressing Emmitt.

He was beginning to move more, which with his babbling made him seem highly, belligerently intoxicated, and though it made dressing far more challenging, I was relieved he was waking up, the drug wearing off.

By the time I had finished dressing him, he was lying facedown on the floor, the lower half of his body in the bathroom, the upper in my office.

Leaving him there, I walked over and sat down behind my desk.

For a moment, I just sat there catching my breath.

In the stillness and silence of the moment, I said a prayerful *thank you*. I was so relieved Anna was okay, so grateful to have her back.

Snatching up the phone, I dialed her desk.

"Classification, Rodden," she said.

"How long before that'll be Jordan?" I asked.

"Too long—even if it was right now," she said.

"We haven't really talked about marriage," I said.

"Seemed premature," she said. "Me not being unmarried yet and all."

"True."

"But I would love to be your wife," she said. "Love

to take your name—something I said I'd never do."

Hearing her say *wife* reminded me of her kidnapper calling her my wife.

"I just called to tell you I love you and that I am so, so, so grateful to have you back."

"You don't know from gratitude," she said. "I . . . I really thought . . . Anyway, I'm even more grateful."

"It's not a competition," I said, "but you're not."

"Am too."

"Are not."

"Am too."

"Hate to change the subject when the current one is so profound," I said, "but . . . the kidnapper kept referring to you as my wife. He seemed to know so much about us, but he kept getting that wrong. Any idea why? Did they both do it?"

"The main one, the one who kept calling you, he did. He called me your wife and you my husband. The other guy never said a word to me and barely a word to the caller. The third guy didn't say anything to anyone."

"Any ideas why?" I asked. "I mean, he's only wrong technically, but . . . did he say anything else that was technically wrong? Anything else that might give us some insight into who he was or why he did it?"

"I've been thinking about it. I have some ideas. I'm also gathering up some info on Cardigan and the Reggie Dalton case. Let me finish up, then we'll talk about all of it face to face."

When we hung up, I picked up the phone again and dialed the control room.

"What can I do you for, Chaplain?" Randy Wayne asked.

"Need an outside line."

"Number?"

I gave it to him. "Emmitt is feeling bad again. It's much worse this time. I'm gonna call his wife to come get him. Okay if I get her to pull up close to the control room?"

"No problem."

"And I may need a hand helping him out."

"Just let me know. I'll send someone."

"Thanks."

Emmitt's wife on the way, I began the arduous task of helping him up and out of the institution.

"Can you stand?" I asked.

He mumbled something.

I lifted his arm and pulled. "Come on. Let's get you up and out of here."

He made what could be described as an incremental move toward standing, but it didn't result in much.

Straddling him, I reached around his chest and heaved.

When I pulled him up, he made no effort to help or stand on his own, so I put him back down again.

Though he had a thick, stocky build, he weighed even more than he looked like he would.

I decided to call for help.

Stumbling over to my desk, I sat back down behind it.

"I guess I never realized just how heavy you are," I said. "Probably because your wife is so large."

In the tradition of Deep South rural route Pentecostal women, Dorcas Emerson dwarfed her husband and eclipsed the three chubby kids continually orbiting around her.

I called the control room.

"I am going to need help with him this time," I said.

"Just sit tight, Chaplain," Randy Wayne said. "I'll have someone down there directly."

Merrill's mom used *directly* like that, but I hadn't heard many other people do it.

"Thank you."

Chapter Thirty-five

"**W**hat're you up to?"

This was the first thing out of Rachel Peterson's mouth when I answered the phone, and it wasn't the casual form of the question.

"Why'd you call and ask about my case?" she added.

"I told you."

"Is my witness in danger?" she asked.

"Is he your witness?"

"Answer me first."

"I think he could be. Tell me what's going on. Please."

"It's simple. Reggie Dalton was murdered. The officers who did it not only disabled cameras and erased footage, they actually re-created the incident using a different inmate after Dalton was dead."

"Cardigan?"

"Cardigan. I mean, he hasn't said so, but . . . I know that's what happened, and I'm pretty close to being able to prove it. Gotta hella video expert from FDLE workin' on the footage. It'd really help to have Cardigan's testimony, but the dumb little bastard still thinks the desperate killers he helped are going to help him."

"Might not after tonight," I said.

"Why? What happened tonight?"

"Something spooked him," I said. "Something said or done has him questioning his options. Be a good time to talk to him."

"I planned to first thing in the morning anyway. I'm trusting you more than I do most people by telling you all this. Am I wrong to?"

"No."

"I hope not."

"Are the officers under investigation on administrative leave or suspended pending the outcome of your investigation?"

"I haven't had enough on them for anything like that. Still don't without Cardigan's testimony."

"So they're still here? Working? Could be right now? With access to Cardigan?"

"What could I do?" she said. "Until he decides to play ball, I've got nothing."

"I had him placed in protection tonight," I said.

"Good. That's good."

"Not if any of the officers working it are the ones involved."

I called the control room again.

"Sorry I haven't gotten anyone down to help you yet, Chaplain. Won't be much longer now."

"No problem. I was actually calling with a quick question."

"Shoot," he said.

"Are Marty Perkins, Lewis Milner, or Jack Kirkus working tonight and if so, where?"

"Let's see . . . I'll have to pull the duty roster to be sure, but . . . I know I saw Jack earlier. 'Course that may have been the day shift. It's all runnin' together by now. Let me look it up and call you back."

It didn't take him long to call me back.

"None of the officers you called about are on duty," he said. "Jack worked the day shift. Don't know when the others work. I can find out. Or I can call them in if it's an emergency. What's going on?"

"Nothing. Not an emergency. I'll talk to them the next time they work."

"You sure?"

"Yeah."

"You looking into their case? Helping the new female IG or . . ."

"Thought I might see if I could help, but . . . was just a random thought."

"They're good men. If you or your dad can help them, you should."

"Thanks."

"Let me know if you need anything else. Oh, and Dorcas Emerson just called. Her car won't start. She's waiting for somebody to come jump her off. Can you just stay with him until she gets here? I'll send someone down to help you with him then. Unless I need to call an ambulance."

"No, that's fine. I'll be here. Thanks."

When we hung up, I called Anna again.

"I can't stand being away from you any longer," I said.

"Feel the same way. I'll head up there in a minute."

"I'll meet you outside," I said. "How are you feeling?"

"Good, actually. Surprisingly so."

"See you in a sec," I said. "Love you."

When Anna stepped out of the front door of her building, I was waiting there for her, gazing up at the red glowing orb in the night-shrouded sky.

Something about the ember-like circle of the moon reminded me of an image I had seen in a film at some point—the pulsating end of a cigarette being smoked by an unseen watcher in the woods on a cold, coal-black night.

After embracing, both of our heads drifted up again, pulled as if the sea itself by the force of the moon.

"I've never seen anything like it," she said. "It's incredible."

We stood there for a moment, gazing up, taking it in, trancelike, mesmerized.

She reached over and grabbed my hand.

"You are my blood," she said.

I was, and she was mine.

I reached over and touched the small, now nearly invisible scar on the right side of her neck. It was the wound from which so much of her blood had been shed, the wound that saved my life, the wound that enabled me to save hers.

That had been so long ago now. If it's true that all the cells in our bodies are replaced every seven years, then my blood was no longer in her, and who she was then she is no longer. But as much as we had become new people since then, we were still and would forever be the same two people who loved each other beyond any description and all explanation—at a level below cellular, beneath molecular.

She is my blood, and always will be.

"I've broken so many vows," I said.

She turned from the moon and looked at me.

"I was just thinking that when you got that scar I had vowed never to use violence again. Which led to a litany of other broken promises, failures, faithlessnesses. I broke an inmate out of prison tonight—and that's not nearly the worst thing I've done since I've been a chaplain. I've lost everything—at least a time or two—including my faith and my sobriety, but I've *never, not ever,* not loved you."

"What you did tonight, you did for me, for love," she said.

I nodded.

"That's a kept vow," she said. "So is your careful use of constrained violence. You're less of a failure and the most faithful of anyone I know. No, you don't break vows, you keep them. Not always in easy or obvious ways, but you do. And all of that is not to say that what you said about never not loving me was lost on me. It wasn't. And the same is true of me for you."

We embraced again.

"Everything else can wait," I said. "Let's go home. Let's make love in our bed and sleep in each other's arms."

She pulled something from her pocket. A small scrap of paper. "I came across something while in my office. So much online pertaining to the moon tonight. I wrote it down so I could read it to you. It's by Tahereh Mafi. 'The moon is a loyal companion. It never leaves. It's always there, watching, steadfast, knowing us in our light and dark moments, changing forever just as we do. Every day it's a different version of itself. Sometimes weak and wan, sometimes strong and full of light. The moon understands what it means to be human. Uncertain. Alone. Cratered by imperfections.'"

"Cratered by imperfections," I repeated. "I really like that."

"You are my moon," she said. "My blood. My moon."

"Shakespeare was wrong about the moon," I said.

"About it being inconstant . . . envious . . . what else?"

"Sick and pale with grief," I said.

"He so was. I prefer the moon."

"'Yours is the light by which my spirit's born,'" I said, quoting Cummings. "'You are my sun, my moon, and all my stars.'"

Chapter Thirty-six

"I looked into Cardigan's case," Anna said.

We were walking up the upper compound toward the chapel beneath the blood moon.

The night had the same ethereal quality as earlier, only more so. It was cooler now with an occasional light breeze, but mostly it was still.

Stillness and silence and something else, a resonance, a presence, as if the blood moon had cast a spell on everything and everyone beneath it.

"Whatta you think?"

"I actually remember it. We talked about it in one of my law classes. Judge Terry Lewis was a guest speaker. Wouldn't comment on the case—even though it wasn't before him and wouldn't be—but we discussed the legal issues surrounding it. The adjunct teaching the class used to be in the same firm as Chris. He represented Cardigan. Wouldn't comment directly either. He's a good attorney. Did a good job with the case. There was no evidence Cardigan had ever even been inside the victim's—Ashley Fountain—side of the duplex. Even more suspicious, none of his prints were on any of her stuff he was supposed to have stolen—not even the things he was believed to be using."

"Were there any prints on her stolen stuff?"

"Three distinct sets including hers, and there were lots in her townhouse, but none of them belonged to Cardigan. And guess how they got onto him in the first place."

"How?"

"Anonymous tip. Somebody drops a dime on him while he's in school and he's arrested when he gets home."

"If he is innocent, and what's happening to him now is related to that, why now? Why wait so long to . . . whatever they were trying to do?"

"No idea," she said. "But there's more. You're gonna love this. Guess who lives in their neighborhood and actually gave a statement to the police during the investigation?"

"Who?"

"Your old father-in-law, Tom corruption-is-my-name raising-crazy-daughters-is-my-game Daniels."

"*Really?*"

"Yeah. Why?"

"Something he said to me recently."

"You've spoken to him?" she asked, surprised.

I nodded. "Just a couple of days ago."

"In case the kidnappers killed me," she said. "Trying to repair the damages in case you want to get back with Susan?"

"I'm not even going to respond to that," I said.

"Good."

"I *am* going to think about how Tom Daniels fits into all this, though."

"Much better use of that big brain of yours," she said. "What else?"

I told her what Rachel Peterson had said.

"Far more likely to be connected to that," she said. "Right?"

"I would think, but . . ."

"Are the officers involved still working here? Is he in protective custody? Do we need to—"

"He is," I said. "Because they are. I had the captain lock him up for tonight. Perkins, Milner, nor Kirkus are working tonight. I should check on Cardigan before we go. Do you mind?"

"Of course not."

We reached the chapel and walked inside.

When we entered my office, we could see that Emmitt had moved some, maybe a few feet, but he was still facedown on the floor.

"I called for his wife, but she got held up. Should be here soon."

We collapsed into the chairs, emotionally exhausted, physical spent.

"I'm so tired," I said.

"Me too."

"And I have to babysit Emmitt and I need to check on Cardigan and I know you're beyond weary and you're eight months pregnant . . . but I don't know how much longer I can wait."

"I feel the same way," she said.

"Part of what makes you perfect."

"We've never done it in your office. Hell, we've never done it at work. And we can't now because of him." She nodded toward Emerson.

"Even with him unconscious, I wouldn't want him in the room," I said.

"So where?"

"The only obvious place," I said. "The sanctuary."

"Really? You'd be willing to do it in there?"

"Willing?"

"I just mean . . . you wouldn't feel like it was inappropriate or . . . that we were defiling it somehow?"

"Just the opposite. It will be the most sacred act I ever commit in there."

With that, we stood, and I led her into the chapel. Closing the door behind us, it was just the two of us in the darkness.

Taking her hand, I led her over to the far side as our eyes adjusted.

On the backside of what was now our sanctuary, I laid her down on the floor between the pews and the windows, beyond which was nothing but blackness—field, fence, and forest, in a pool of blood-red moonlight, and we made love in a way that could only be described as an act of faith.

Chapter Thirty-seven

"**H**ave I ever told you how much I love prison?" Anna said.

I laughed. "It *is* sort of *our* place," I said.

"It is, isn't it? Of course, now every place is our place."

"True."

We were walking across the front of the chapel toward my office, holding hands, taking our time.

"I'm not nearly as in a rush to get home now if you want to work on the case some more," she said.

"Let's go home and do that again in our bed."

The phone started ringing on my desk.

Releasing her hand, I removed the keys from my pocket and unlocked and opened the door.

Instead of following me in, she sat on the end of the front pew closest to my office door.

"Chaplain Jordan."

"What the hell is goin' on there?" Rachel Peterson said.

"Whatta you mean?"

"You tried to help Ronald Cardigan escape?"

"What?"

"Is that why you called me about him? I can't believe

I told you all I did. I thought you were—"

"What're you talkin' about?" I asked.

"You can't worm your way out of this one," she said. "Not with so many witnesses. Not with a—"

The line went dead.

"Rachel?"

When I heard the dial tone, I hung up.

"What is it?" Anna asked from the doorway behind me.

From the floor in front of my desk, Emmitt moaned something.

"It's not good," I said, and called the control room.

When Randy Wayne answered I said, "Need an outside line. Calling the IG. It's an emergency."

"Number."

"You have it," I said. "I called her earlier this evening."

"That's right. Let me see . . ."

"I'll call you back with info as soon as I finish. Okay?"

"Nah."

"Huh?"

"Nah. It's not okay."

"What do you—"

"She knows everything she needs to."

"*You?*" I said. "You're involved in this?"

"Why you think I got Pine to lie to get you back in? Why do you think I'm workin' tonight? You think you fooled anybody dressin' that convict up in Emmitt Emerson's clothes?"

I thought about how disheveled and out of breath he had been when we reentered the institution tonight. Was it because he had just run back from the woods between the prison and Potter Farm?

"What does she know?" I asked. "What does she think she knows?"

"That you tried to help an inmate escape tonight. 'Course, by the time she gets here, you'll be dead so she'll only have our story. I've got to tell you . . . you think you're so smart, but I've got you beat. Not only did you attempt to help an inmate escape, not only were you killed by that same inmate before we killed him, but all this happened while the three suspects in the Dalton case are nowhere near the prison."

I didn't say anything, just thought.

"I can tell you all this," he said, "I can tell you anything . . . because you're locked in my prison and can't get out. There's a reason they call this the control room. Guess who has complete control over your ass right now? Guess! It's smiling, friendly Randy Wayne 'Have a nice day' Davis. That's who. You're in the empty upper compound of a maximum security prison with no weapons and no way out. Think about it."

Now that he had removed his mask, I thought back to all the little toxic leaks I had witnessed him exhibit over the past year, all the ways the man behind the mask had peeked out.

"None of this is part of the plan, but the plan didn't go as . . . ah . . . planned. So some improvising is called for. If he doesn't like it, well . . . he shouldn't have fucked up his part of the original plan. Am I right? Come on. I'm right, right?"

What Tom Daniels had said popped into my head. *You son of a bitch. You know, don't you? I knew it. I told them you—*

Was Daniels the *he* Randy Wayne was referring to? Was he somehow behind all this?

"'Course if he's dead he don't really have a say anymore, does he? Am I being unreasonable? You can tell me if I am."

Was he talking about Karl Jason? Maybe Jason was really behind all this and not just an actor playing a part.

Anna made a sudden little noise, an intake of breath, a wordless sound that communicated plenty.

I spun around and looked out my side door into the sanctuary.

Ronnie Cardigan was behind her, holding a sharp shank to her neck, its tip touching the small scar I had been touching just a little earlier.

"I'm real sorry, Chaplain. I don't want this any more than you do, but . . ."

"Is he there? Man I wish I could see the look on your face," Randy Wayne said. "Who's smarter than John Jordan? Who is? Who?"

I dropped the phone onto the desk and eased out into the sanctuary.

It was dark, the only light at all coming through the glass panels of the entry doors and the narrow strip from my partially open office door.

"Ronnie," I said, my voice soft, calm, but pleading, "just wait. Don't do anything you can't undo."

"Too late for that."

"It's not. Not yet. Listen to me. Think about what you're doin'. You're holding a weapon to the throat of and threatening an innocent pregnant woman. She's eight months pregnant. Think about what you're doin'."

"I don't have a choice."

"You do. You absolutely do. Just hear me out. Okay?"

"Talk fast," he said.

"I don't know what they promised you, but they'll

never let you do this and live. They're getting you to kill us and then they'll kill you. Pin everything on you and maybe some on us. We die. They skate."

He seemed to think about that.

"I can help you. We can get out of this. We can work together and bring them down and stay alive in the process."

He shook his head. "No way. Maybe I shouldn't be doing this. And maybe they'll kill me even if I do, but . . . no way we walk."

"We can."

"You don't even know who it is or how many."

"I will if you tell me what you know, if you let me in on what's goin' on."

"I lied to you about what I did," he said. "I took an occasional night class, but I wasn't a full-time student or anything like that. My part-time job was a cover. I . . . I dealt a little. I didn't steal any of that bitch's shit, but the product was mine—at least most of it. Guess some was hers. Thing is, keeping so much in my place like that . . . I had a surveillance system. I'm good with shit like that. My uncle has a security business and I worked for him for a while. Whoever killed her had to be on my system. Shit goes down, cops crawling around everywhere, I decide best thing for me to do is walk away. Before I can look at the footage or pull my shit together or get the hell out of Dodge, I'm being arrested. Now, nobody in here knows me, knows my skill set. Hell, when they confiscated all my shit, my surveillance equipment wasn't part of it. Long gone. Bye bye. So how does anyone in here know I know my way around a system? Tell me that. But when these bastards want help with their surveillance situation, who do they come see? How do they know? Tell me that. Had to be Ashley's killer. No one else knows. So what's that mean?

He one of them? He another inmate in here trying to cut a deal for himself? What?"

"You fixed the footage for them," I said.

"Best I could, given my time and equipment constraints."

"And they tried to kill you tonight," I said. "Think about it. You did what they asked and they tried to kill you. Whatta you think's gonna happen if you help them this time?"

"Same thing."

"Let Anna go. Put down the weapon. Help me get us out of this."

"I'm gonna let her go," he said. "But don't try anything."

"I won't. I promise. Just lower the—"

The power in the chapel went off.

Randy Wayne had also killed most of the exterior lights in the upper compound.

Darkness.

Now with no light spilling into the sanctuary from my office or the hallway, deep dimness was now blackness, and the only thing even slightly resembling illumination was the red glow coming from the far side windows.

"They're coming," Ronnie said. "We're all gonna die."

"Just let Anna go and let's talk about it," I said.

"I have," he said.

"He has," Anna said.

We stepped forward, feeling for each other in the darkness.

When I had her, I guided her behind me and called to Ronnie.

"Come on," I said. "We can go out the back. Walk

toward the red glow over there."

"Way ahead of you," he said.

His voice came from over by the back door, near where just a few minutes ago Anna and I had made love.

I led her toward the same spot, pulling her more quickly than I would've liked, but believing Ronnie was right and we didn't have much time.

Ronnie jerked on the door.

"It's locked," he said.

"I know. I'll unlock it in just a second."

As we neared the door, I stopped short and whispered to Anna to stay there.

"Hand me the shank," I said to Ronnie when I reached the door.

"No way. It's all I got."

"Then back up several steps while I unlock the door."

He did.

When I had the door unlocked, he started walking toward me.

"Let's talk about what we're gonna do," I said. "Make a plan that gives us the best—"

"Better if we split up," he said.

When he reached the door, he paused and said, "Good luck."

"You too."

"If somethin' happens to me . . ."

"Yeah?"

Anna was behind me now.

"There's another camera in my place I guarantee the killer didn't find. In case you make it and I don't. I didn't kill Ashley. Don't let whoever did get away with it."

A noise from the hallway let us know someone was there.

Ronnie took off.

"Ready?" I whispered to Anna.

"Do I have a choice?"

Chapter Thirty-eight

Beneath the blood moon.

Running.

Toward the greenhouse.

All around us dark, moist grass for what seemed like miles.

A deep, dense fog had rolled in, shrouding the compound, blocking out the few points of light remaining, making it even more difficult to see.

Between the chapel and the perimeter fence was nearly two hundred yards. Behind us the chapel and the visiting park, the control room and the perimeter fence, beyond which was Admin, parking lots, training, and the only road leading to and from the institution. Before us, out in the open field, an overgrown greenhouse. A good ways beyond it, Laundry, Medical, Classification, Psychology, and Confinement. Beyond them, the inside fence that separated the upper and lower compounds.

Anna let go of my hand.

I stopped and turned.

"Don't stop," she said. "Keep moving. I'm here. I'll stay with you, but I have to use both hands to hold my stomach."

"Sorry. Are you okay?"

"One thing at a time. Let's get somewhere safe, then we'll . . ."

I started moving again, slower this time.

"Let's just get to the greenhouse," I said. "We'll regroup. Rest a minute. Make a plan."

I was guessing they wanted our deaths to look like the work of inmates. That meant we'd have to be stabbed or beaten to death—both of which meant whoever did it would have to get close to us to do it.

Even if they could see us on this dark night, they probably wouldn't fire on us—something that could not only not be blamed on an inmate but would draw attention to what was going on—unless as a final, desperate, last resort.

I had no way of knowing how many officers were involved, but my guess was no more than a few. They would need to keep this quiet and take us out as quickly as possible.

Was Tom Daniels behind this somehow? Was he pulling the levers from an unseen vantage point? If so, being able to take out Anna too, especially with her pregnant, had to be a special kind of sweet, twisted revenge for him. Susan, his daughter and my wife at the time, had had been pregnant when, because of his crimes, she left me and aborted the only part of me, of us, of any evidence there had ever been an us—something they both had taunted me with.

Slowing.

Nearing the greenhouse.

Scanning the area.

Darkness in darkness, surrounded by darkness.

I couldn't make out anything but the red-tinged tin roof, its dew-wet surface adding to the illusion that the rust had taken on an incandescent quality.

When we reached the backside of the building, I helped Anna down to the ground, then sat beside her, each of us propping our backs against the polyethylene walls.

"Are you okay?" I asked. "I'm so sorry about all this."

"I'm fine. Stop worrying about me and let's figure out how to get out of here."

"There's probably lots of contraband in the greenhouse," I said, "but it'd take too long to find it. Was anyone in Medical when you were down there?"

"Entire building was empty. Both sides."

The building held Medical on one side and Psychology and Classification on the other.

"We could call for help if we could get to someone who Randy Wayne would give an outside line to. Even someone with a radio would—"

"Bill Sayles," she said, blurting the name of one of her more colorful Classification coworkers.

"Yeah?"

"Keeps saying the lunatics are going to take over the asylum eventually, that it's just a matter of time until we have our own Attica. Either that or some sort of shooting by a crazy officer like at Fort Hood."

"Okay."

"So he snuck in a cell phone," she said. "It's in his desk. Only a matter of time before it's found and confiscated, but unless it happened within the last few days while I was gone, it should still be there."

"Thank God for Bill's paranoia. Make sure you still have the keys."

She felt her pockets for them.

"Shit."

"Not there?"

"No."

Without her keys we couldn't get in the building, let alone Bill's office.

"They could be on the chapel floor or anywhere on the ground between here and there."

"Sorry."

"Other options," I said. "Think. We could try to get the attention of the guard in Tower II."

"Assuming he's not in on it," she said, "we'd draw the attention of our, ah, pursuers too. They'd get to us before he could get down out of the tower. And no way he'd fire at other officers just because we yelled up they were after us—and that's if he could hear us. And if he radios anyone, it'll be the control room. Randy Wayne will just make up some bullshit story. Hell, he may even convince him to fire down at *us*."

"If we could just figure out a really good hiding place, we could stay hidden until morning when other officers and staff arrived. It'd be far better for you and the baby."

"But if they found us, we'd be dead. Couldn't run."

"Why it'd have to be the perfect spot," I said.

"Can you think of any?" she asked.

"Not so far."

"Me either."

"We need to keep moving," I said.

"Where?"

I shook my head. "I'm not sure."

"Okay. Wait," she said, as she started to push herself up.

"What is it? The baby?"

"The keys. They were on the ground beside me. Must have slid out of my pocket when I sat down."

I helped her up and kissed her.

"Where to?" she said.

"Back door of Classification," I said.

I looked around. Saw nothing. And we were off again.

No matter which direction we ran, no matter how our course shifted and corrected, we always seemed to be facing the glowing red orb.

Unbidden, a line of Robert Frost came to mind. *We ran as if to meet the moon.*

Chapter Thirty-nine

Moving toward Classification. Feeling our way through the fog.

Slower now.

Darkness. Difficult to see.

Eerie red glow on the edges of the fog.

Occasional security light in the distance. Weak. Wan. There, then gone.

Tension.

Who was watching us? Was someone there in the fog? Coiled? About to strike?

Deal with it when it happens. Keep moving.

Behind me, Anna's breathing sounded bad. I knew she was scared and in pain, and there was nothing I could do.

To occupy my mind, I made a mental list of what we needed to do and gather up in Classification. I went through what I thought might be in there and how we might use it.

Finally, we reached the back door.

As we stood there, scanning the area and unlocking the door, we could see Confinement on the other side of the fence that separated the two buildings.

"Someone will certainly be in there," she said.

"True, but we can't even get to the building, let alone inside."

"Maybe we could get their attention somehow."

She unlocked and opened the door. I looked inside, then we were in, the door closed and locked behind us.

Pausing a minute before we continued, I tried to get a sense if anyone else was in the dark hallway.

"Should I turn on the light?" she asked.

"I don't think so. Which office is his?"

"Last on the right. It's a double. He shares it with Fredericka."

"You okay?"

"I'm okay."

"Stay close. Can I hold your hand?"

"Please."

The long, narrow corridor had empty sheetrock walls, a tile floor, and offices off each side. Like every other part of the prison save the personal space of staff offices, it held nothing decorative, no clutter, no random objects of any kind.

It was a clear, straight shot and we felt our way through it, moving slowly, cautiously.

"I'm scared," she whispered.

I squeezed her hand a little tighter. "We're almost there."

"Randy Wayne knows I have keys to Classification. They'll come here when they don't find us in the chapel."

"Let's try to be gone before they get here," I said.

Finally, we reached the door and she unlocked it.

"You find the phone," I said. "I'll search both desks and work areas for anything else we can use."

While she rummaged through Bill's desk, I did the same across from her in Fredericka's.

"Please let her be a smoker," I said.

"She is," Anna said without looking up.

We had left the lights off and were using the little illumination streaming in the window from a security lamp next to the first dorm on the lower compound, but it was far in the distance and blanketed by fog so mostly what we were doing was feeling our way through the drawers.

I found two lighters and a few packs of matches, a small can of hairspray, a nail file, some bobbie pins, a couple of bite-size Snickers bars, an orange, a couple of paperback romances, a few random keys, tape, some paperclips, a deck of cold case playing cards, rubber bands, and Band-Aids.

"She doesn't have any shoes over there, does she?" Anna asked.

"No. Why?"

"Lost mine while we were running and my feet are killing me."

"So sorry, baby. I had no idea. Any in your office?"

"I'm sure I have something."

"Any progress over there?"

"Haven't found the phone yet, but here's a MoonPie."

Something rattled under Bill's desk.

"Wait," she said. "What is this? Oh, Bill, you beautiful paranoid little man."

"What is it?"

"Baseball bat," she said. "Must have snagged it from the rec yard."

"Score."

"He had it taped underneath his desk. But no phone."

"Really? Have you already gone through every drawer?"

"Pretty much, yeah, but . . ."

"Nothing it could be in?"

"That's what I'm checking now. This bag of potato chips isn't crunching the right way."

I stood and felt my way around the rest of the room.

"Bingo," she said.

"Got it."

"Yep. Shit. It's dead. *Fuck*."

"Is there a potato chip covered charger in there?"

"No. Damn it man. Really thought that was our— wait. No. Here. Here it is. This is it. Has to be. Plug it in or bring it with us?"

I stepped to the door and looked out into the darkness.

"Hand me the bat and plug it in."

Chapter Forty

The phone had charged for no more than a minute when the electricity went off.

"Time to motor," I said. "Bring the charger. We'll find a place with power."

A phone from down the hall started ringing.

"That's mine," she said.

From somewhere in the building a door clanged shut, the sound of its heavy metal impact reverberating down the hard-surfaced corridors.

Emergency backup lights blinked on in the institutional hallways.

Though still dim, there was at least now some visibility.

"Whatta we do?" Anna whispered.

I looked through the narrow pane of glass in both directions—the exit we had entered through and the door opposite it but closer to us now that led to Psychology.

"Hadn't we better move now? John?"

"I'm thinking. Just a—"

A young white inmate with prison tats on his hands, neck, and part of his face—the only areas of his skin exposed—walked through the door connecting to Psychology carrying the largest, longest prison knife I had ever seen.

It was over a foot in length with an extremely sharp blade that gleamed even in the very low light, its handle a wrap of white athletic tape, on which were drawn black felt-tip swastikas.

"Get down behind the desk," I whispered to Anna, trying to block out the image of that cold, cruel weapon running through her and her unborn child.

She did.

I backed away from the window to an angle where I could remain unseen while seeing him as he passed by.

The pale, inked inmate was part of the Aryan Brotherhood or some other group like it—or would be once he iced us.

Gangs like them made up less than one tenth of one percent of the prison population but accounted for some thirty percent of murders committed inside.

His head was scabbed and skinned, still bleeding in spots, his face scarred and pocked and acne ravaged.

I didn't recognize him, but I knew him. Knew his mindset and mentality, knew his unreasonableness and rage, knew his lack of empathy, compassion, or even conscience.

After he had passed by, I slid closer to the window again.

The outer door at the other end of the hall, the one Anna and I had entered, opened and two officers walked in, their radios squawking.

One of the men was Pine. I couldn't see the other man because he was behind the behemoth.

"Anything?" Pine asked.

"Ain't seen shit."

Pine radioed Control.

"No sign of 'em here," he said.

"Tell Butler to search the building room by room—
and to be thorough. You take Cantor back outside and set
him loose."

"Ten-four."

"If Butler finds them, tell him to radio you and you
bring Cantor back in."

"Copy that," he said into the radio, then to the two
present, "You heard the man."

Pine then turned and unlocked the door behind him
and he and Cantor walked out, leaving Butler alone in the
hallway.

Beginning with the first door on his left, Butler
unlocked it, crouched in a defensive position, reached in
and turned on the light, looked around, then walked in, the
door falling shut behind him.

"What's goin' on?" Anna said.

I told her.

"Whatta we do?"

"Either try to sneak out while he's searching one
of the offices or jump him when he comes in this one. Or
something I haven't thought of but you have."

"No, that seems like our only two options."

"Which one you think we should try?"

"There is no try. Just do or do not do," she said.

"Which one do you think we should *do*, Mr. Miyagi?"

"Not for me to say, Daniel-san. You must decide."

"Think I'll watch him a little longer first," I said.

"Very wise Daniel-san. Make Miyagi proud."

Though he had used a lot of caution entering the
room, Butler walked out normally.

As he got closer and I could make him out more, I
recognized him. Last year he was involved in an incident on
an outside grounds crew where an inmate was tied to a tree
and beaten. Though severely beaten, the inmate survived

and ultimately recovered. Three of the five officers involved were fired and were awaiting trial. Butler was one of the two who were neither charged nor fired. He and the other officer claimed to not have been involved and to have actually tried to stop it. So far neither the inmate involved nor the other three officers had given contradictory evidence. Perhaps he had cut a deal and his involvement here tonight was part of the payment.

"Whatta you think?" Anna asked.

"There's no way to know how long he'll be in any given room. Some he comes right back out, others he's a minute or more. He enters cautiously but exits casually."

"Ah ha," she said.

"Ah ha?"

"Miyagi think best time to brain with bat."

Waiting.

Officer Butler was in the office two doors down from the one I had been in with Anna just a few moments before.

He had entered some thirty seconds ago and I was waiting for him to come out, hoping no one else showed up from either end of the hall and saw me.

Anna was still hiding behind Bill's desk. Waiting until the unpleasantness was over, which I hoped would be soon.

I heard or sensed movement behind the door, maybe even a passing shadow on the floor.

I hadn't played baseball since junior high and wasn't any good even back then, but I gripped the bat like a minor leaguer who had just made it to the Show, and prepared to swing for the fences.

His hand on the handle . . .

Batter, batter, batter.

The door beginning to open.

Batter, batter, batter.

Open now, him stepping out.

Batter, batter, batter, SWING batter.

My swing took too long. Seeing it coming, he had stepped back and held his hands up, his arms taking the brunt of the blow.

Hesitating a moment, but only a moment, I stepped up and shoved him into the room, bringing the bat up again.

He fell to the floor and began backing up in a kind of broken-arm crab crawl.

Not wanting to hit him in the face, I brought the bat up above me and down on the top of his head.

He tried to lift his injured arms to ward off the blow but was too late.

Trying to hit him hard enough to knock him out but not so hard as to do any lasting damage, my conflicted swing was weaker than it should have been, hard enough to stun him but not to knock him out.

He slumped down, completely still for a moment, then eventually began to reach for his radio.

Before he could depress the button on the mic clipped to his shoulder, I swung the bat, hitting him on the side of the head and this time knocking him out.

As quickly as I could, I gathered his cuffs and keys and radio and belt and gloves and lighter, turned off the light in the office, and went to get Anna.

Chapter Forty-one

"**A**re you okay?" Anna asked.

I nodded.

She was standing near the door waiting on me when I came back into Bill and Fredericka's office.

"Sure?"

I nodded again.

"Where to?"

"Whatta you think?" I asked.

"Somewhere close. Somewhere to hide. Somewhere with power."

"Wonder if they cut the power to this entire building or just this side?"

"Doesn't matter," she said. "This key won't get us into Medical."

"So wherever we go to get power, we'll have to break in. Not something I'm sure we can do, or *if* we can do, do quietly enough to avoid detection."

"Should we just hide here? How long do you think we'd have to make it?"

"I think there's a possibility Rachel Peterson is on her way," I said. "If so, and if she can actually get in, and they can't convince her we're not here or distract her with other things, I'd say about an hour and a half. If we have to wait for the first employees to arrive . . . Shift change is not until seven, but . . . someone who works in Food Services comes in early to supervise breakfast, right? If Rachel doesn't come tonight or doesn't even know to look for us, I'd say between three and four hours."

"That's a very long time to survive in here like this," she said.

"Not for two badasses like us," I said.

She smiled, but tears appeared in her eyes. "I notice there's no blood on your bat, badass," she said. "You tried not to hurt him, just knock him out, didn't you?"

"It's possible I'm not completely clear on the definition."

We fell silent a moment and I thought about our options.

Psychology was just one hallway on this side of the building, which meant the electricity was most likely off in it too. Medical was on the other side of this same building, Laundry on the other side of it. Both would have to be broken into—something I didn't think we had the tools to do. And even if we did, we'd most likely be spotted before we could get in.

Food Services was directly across the asphalt road from where we were now. Moving toward it would make us visible to Tower II and exposed to everyone for a longer period of time, and it too would have to be broken into. But it was larger with more places to hide—even on the exterior of the building, the back of which held a loading dock, a cinderblock wall cleaning area, and a fenced-in trash pile, and was littered with empty trays and racks and other random items.

If I could break the lock on the gate to the trash pile, I could hide Anna inside. If I could break into

Laundry, I could hide her beneath the clothes in one of the many large canvas laundry carts. If I had wings and could fly, I could soar us out of here to safety.

"Anything?" Randy Wayne asked.

His voice coming through the radio sounded like he was in the room.

"Let's go," I said to Anna.

I double-checked the hallway in both directions, then opened the door and led her out.

As we walked down the hallway toward the back door, I pulled my shirt up in front of my mouth, depressed the button on the mic, and spoke into it, hoping the muffling from the shirt and the echoing of the hallway would help disguise my deception.

"Nothin' so far," I said softly with slightly more of a Southern accent than I normally had. "'Bout halfway through."

"Let me know. And speed it up a bit, man. Clock's tickin'."

"Will do."

As we neared the back door, I could hear a key being inserted into it from the other side.

"Here," I whispered.

I turned to the door on my right, unlocked it, and led her inside.

I was fairly certain they had the back door open and were in the hallway with more than enough time to see or hear what we had just done. I stepped to the side of the door, moved Anna behind me, and readied the bat.

And waited.

"BUTLER," Pine yelled. "WHERE YOU AT?"

From the side of the narrow pane of glass, I watched as Pine Tree lumbered up the hallway alone.

I thought about our options.

Try to sneak out when he gets far enough away. Of course, he'd probably hear us—if not coming out of this door then trying to unlock and open the other.

Attack him with the bat. Of course, he'd probably just take it away from me, pick his teeth with it, then squash me.

We could stay put. Hide here while he discovers the body, confirms we're here, and radios for help. Of course, they'd find us in no time and there would be more of them to deal with—including Cantor and his sword.

"We've got to sneak out," I said. "Best chance is when he goes into the office where Butler is."

"Okay."

"Here," I said, handing her the key. "You unlock the outer door. I'm sure you can do it more quietly than I can. I'll be watching the hallway to see if he hears us."

I watched as Pine neared the office that held Butler.

As he continued down the hallway, looking into each office, he periodically called out for Butler but he only looked over his shoulder once.

"Here we go," I said as he neared the fateful office. "Quickly and quietly."

When he reached the door, looked in, and saw Butler, he pulled out his keys and rushed inside.

"Now," I said.

Chapter Forty-two

As we stepped back out into the black night, Pine's voice came through Butler's radio.

"They're here," Pine said, voice pitched high, words coming fast. "Classification. Butler's down."

"Scotty, get over there," Randy Wayne said. "Now. Whatta you mean, down? How bad is he?"

"He ain't conscious."

"Leave him for now. Search the building. Find them."

"They got his radio."

"Motherfuck Almighty," Randy Wayne said. "An unarmed preacher and a bitch about to have a baby."

"We prefer *badasses*," Anna whispered.

I laughed.

We were running back the same way we had come earlier, behind Medical, toward Laundry.

"I'm being literal here," Randy Wayne was saying. "An actual human being baby could drop out of her shit-don't-stink better-than-thou pristine pussy any second now. How haven't you taken care of them yet?"

"Did you know any of that about me?" Anna asked.

"Sure, but only because we've been intimate. How does he know?"

"Think he hates all women or just me?"

We reached the end of Medical and paused for a moment. I looked around. We'd be more exposed as we crossed between Medical and Laundry.

"Okay," I said. "Just to the back edge of Laundry. Ready?"

"Say the word and I'll move my pristine little pussy just as fast as I can."

"On three," I said. "Three."

We took off.

Stepping onto the asphalt pad, I cringed for Anna's feet, the long, shapely, tender feet I found so sexy. I had to find something for her to wear. My shoes were too big and would come off as soon as she tried to run. Maybe I could find a pair of inmate sneakers in Laundry that would fit her.

Just as we reached the back corner of the laundry building, I saw Scotty Branson, the officer Randy Wayne had told to get to Classification, round the corner where we had just been standing a few moments before.

He paused for a moment, just as we had, and turned and looked over his shoulder toward us.

We stood perfectly still in the darkness, our backs pressed up against the cinderblock wall.

The night was still deathly quiet, the blood moon still a deep, dark red. Everything was still shrouded in fog and a burgundy-tinged blackness.

He appeared to be looking directly at us.

Could he see us? Did he know we were here?

Eventually, he looked away, scanning other directions, then continuing to the back door of Classification and going in.

I turned the radio back up slightly and held it to my ear.

". . . called futility, John," Randy Wayne was saying. "Understand? All you're doin' is delaying the inevitable. You have nowhere to go. No chance of escape. No way to call for help. No weapons. No hope. You don't even have the radio. In just a second, we're goin' to switch to another channel, then from there alternate between channels at intervals you couldn't possibly guess even if you were fuckin' Rain Man. So why don't y'all make it easy on all of us and turn yourself in? We can work something out. Nobody has to get hurt from all this. Just for once in your life be a team player. Whatta you say?"

I said nothing, just continued scanning the area around us as I listened.

"Come on," he said. "Before Cantor cuts somebody. 'Cause I'm tellin' you, he goes to work on somebody with that big blade of his and parts are gonna fall out that we can't put back in. Vital parts. Know what I mean? That ain't the kind of cesarean you want Anna havin'. Trust me. Or maybe you do. I hear it's not your baby. But, John, buddy, Cantor won't just take the baby. Come on, you know that. He'll rip her too. Rip her good. You gonna put her through that?"

Anna squeezed my hand.

"You ever looked at his jacket?" he said. "Ever read in detail what he's in here for? He won Best with a Blade at the American Sociopathic Association's award show something like five years running."

He cracked himself up with that one and took a moment to enjoy it, laughing and appreciating himself— leaving the microphone on as he did.

"You remember a year or so back, that inmate who

got filleted in F Dorm? Ears cut off and shoved down his throat. Smiley face carved into his belly, his viscera hanging out of its mouth. There was more, but you get the . . . You remember that, right? 'Course you do. Nobody forgets shit like that. Cantor's work. Yeah, boy knows his way around a blade and a body. That's for sure. Thing is, John, I'm gonna make you watch him do that to Anna if you don't stop all this and turn yourself in right now."

I didn't respond.

"Last chance. Offer is going . . . going . . . gone. Okay boys, he chose the hard way. Just like we were hoping he would. Let's make it extra hard, though, 'specially for the stuck up bitch. Switch to our alternate channel and begin switching around in the intervals we discussed in three . . . two . . ."

The radio went silent.

"You okay?" I whispered to Anna.

She nodded.

"It's just bravado," I lied. "Just threats. Just trying to scare us."

"Well, it worked."

"Sorry," I said.

I pulled her to me and held her, continuing to look around us as I did.

"I'm so sorry about all this," I said. "I'm gonna take care of you, get you out of this. You're going to be fine."

"Where to? What next?"

"Was thinking we might double back to the chapel since they've already checked it. Maybe they won't come back to it for a while. We have the keys and can get into any part of it, and I think there's an outlet in the kitchen that works when the emergency lights kick on."

She nodded. "Okay."

"Sorry about your feet. We'll figure something out for them when we get there."

"They're the least of my worries now. The very least."

Chapter Forty-three

I slowly slid the key into the lock and turned the handle on the exterior door that led into the fellowship hall and kitchen. It was in the very back corner of the chapel, directly behind the sanctuary, separated by a removable room divider that folded into each of the side walls.

We entered the empty room, my dew-wet shoes squeaking on the tile floor, and moved toward the kitchen on the far side.

The room was dark, but I could see that the divider was closed and all the chairs and tables were stacked against the walls. We had a clear straight walk to the small back hallway that led to the kitchen.

"You okay back there?" I whispered.

"I am. And I love you."

"I love you."

I opened the back hallway door, which was dimly illuminated by the emergency lamp on the wall near the ceiling—only one side of which was working. It was a small, narrow L-shaped hallway off of which were the inmate and volunteer bathrooms and the kitchen. The kitchen was to our right. It and the volunteer bathroom were the only doors that locked back here.

I unlocked it and we walked inside.

The first thing that stood out to me wasn't the presence but the absence of something. I didn't hear the hum of the refrigerator.

"Hear that?" I asked.

"What?"

"Exactly."

"Oh. No hum."

"Tell you what, I'll still pull out the fridge and you can try all the outlets in here while I go get you some sneakers out of my office and check on Emmitt."

"Just hurry back."

"I will. The fridge could be plugged into the wrong outlet. Just try them all. If you get enough charge, go ahead and call."

"Who?"

"Merrill or Dad or nine-one-one. Nine-one-one will be faster and easier, but with Dad or Merrill you can really explain what's going on."

"You have either of their numbers?"

I gave them to her as I pulled the refrigerator back from the wall.

Then I hugged and kissed her and hurried away so I could hurry back.

Checking both ways before I opened the kitchen door, I stepped out and took the half dozen or so steps to the door that opened into the main hallway right across from my office. Pausing there, I looked around. Seeing no one, I eased open the door and stepped into the hallway.

But before I could cross the hall to my office, something in the sanctuary caught my eye.

I was seeing it through the square glass windows of the main chapel doors to my left and at first wasn't sure what I was seeing.

Snatching open the door on the right, I stepped into the sanctuary and crossed over to the center aisle and stared in disbelief.

There in the front of the sanctuary, nailed to the podium in a horrific crucifixion pose, was the naked body of Emmitt Emerson.

Blood and bowels hung and dripped out of a large hole in his side. His eyes were missing, their sockets black bloody gaps into which his head could be seen, out of which nothing would ever be seen again. Blood also dripped from his wrists and feet and the jagged cuts across his forehead, this last appearing to mimic the damage that would be caused by a crown of thorns.

The entire terrifying tableau was lit from below by an emergency light that had been ripped from the wall and brought over to give dramatic illumination to the sadistic and sacrilegious scene.

This is my fault. I brought him in. I drugged him. I used him to—

The front door of the chapel opened and I dropped to the floor and rolled beneath the pew nearest me.

When the sanctuary doors opened, I slid a little farther beneath the pew.

"What the fuck?" a voice I didn't recognize said.

"Jesus Christ, man," another voice said. "Is that— Who is that?"

"I have no idea, but I know whose work it is. It's what happens when you let a serial killer loose to play with a big knife. Fuck. Look at it. Better call RW."

One of them radioed Randy Wayne.

"Your boy crucified some poor bastard in the chapel."

"Oh good. Who?"

"Don't recognize him."

"Oh shit. Bet it's Emerson. What's he look like?"

He told him.

"That's him. Oh, well. You know what? Actually, this is good. This is very good. Yeah, this helps with the story."

"Whatta we do?"

"Leave everything just as it is. Keep looking for them."

"Ten-four."

"Oh, and don't get on the wrong end of Cantor's blade."

"Shit's not funny," one of them said.

"It's kinda funny," the other said.

"Let's finish lookin' and get the fuck out of here. That shit's creepin' the fuck out of me."

I could see their boots as they began to move toward me.

If they did a thorough search, they'd see me. There was no way around it.

If they went in the back, they'd see Anna. If I didn't get back to her soon, she'd probably come out looking for me.

They continued toward me, still on the back aisle, staying together, easing their way farther into the sanctuary.

"What if that motherfucker decides to come after us?"

"RW?"

"No. The psychopath with the knife."

"Shoot him."

"With what?"

"You're really wandering around in here in the dark without a weapon?"

"How'd you . . . I didn't know we could bring one in."

"Tonight's different. Nobody but us up here. Who's

gonna know?"

"Where's the captain?"

"RW took care of him. Put something in his coffee. He's sleepin' like a big baby. When he wakes up he'll be one of the ones blamed for all this shit."

"Sweet. Think I can run out to my truck and get my gun?"

"RW ain't gonna let you outta here."

"You got an extra?"

"Just stick close to me. I gotcha."

"Hey, wait. If they were in here, Psycho Slasher would've gotten them."

"Good point. Let's look somewhere else."

They stopped walking.

"I mean, hell, we're here more for containment than anything else. He'll find 'em and fuck 'em up. All we gotta do is lay low and stay alive."

They turned and began walking back the way they had come.

When they reached the sanctuary doors, I raised up to see if they were leaving the building or checking the back hallway.

At first they just stood there.

After a little time had passed, they stepped toward the door, then stopped and started back this way, then stopped again.

They were saying something I couldn't make out.

If they did go down the back hallway toward the kitchen, I'd have to move fast. I wish I knew which one had the gun. I'd need to attack him first. But there was no way for me to know.

In another moment, they headed toward the front door and walked out of the building.

Chapter Forty-four

Back beneath the blood moon.

Bat in one hand, Anna's hand in the other.

Moving quickly, but carefully, making a wide swing around the right side of the upper compound that brought us close to the perimeter fence.

"What about the perimeter patrol?" she said.

The prison was encircled by an asphalt road that was patrolled during each shift by an armed officer in a vehicle. If we stayed near the perimeter fence long enough, he'd eventually drive by.

"I thought about trying to wait out here and get his attention earlier, but figured he'd be working with them. No way Randy Wayne wouldn't have one of his guys out there."

"Maybe," she said. "Or maybe he doesn't have any more guys. Maybe he thought he'd be able to take us out quickly and quietly in the chapel hours ago."

"Maybe," I said. "We can risk it if you think we should."

"Might not have a choice eventually, then it'd be less of a risk."

"How are you feeling?"

She was wearing a pair of sneakers I had in my office, under which were three pairs of thick socks. When

I had returned to the kitchen with them, she was sitting on the floor, her back leaning against one of the cabinets, the front of her pants wet with blood.

In that moment, the fact that none of the kitchen outlets had power became a secondary consideration.

"I'm okay," she said. "Feet much better. Still bleeding some, but can't tell how much. Pain's not too bad. Some in my abdomen. Mostly just achy. I can move faster if we need to."

Suddenly, something was there in front of me, and I tripped. Letting go of Anna's hand so I didn't pull her down with me, I hit the ground and rolled, coming up with the bat as soon as I stopped.

"Chaplain, it's me," Cardigan said. "Don't swing."

"Ronnie?"

"Yeah."

I got to my feet and moved back over to Anna.

"What're you doing out here?"

"This is where I've been the whole time. Thought I'd just lie out here in the dark and wait for daybreak and shift change or . . . I didn't know what else to do."

Something Lao Tzu said popped into my head. *In dwelling, live close to the ground. In thinking, keep to the simple. In conflict, be fair and generous.*

I had listened to the *Tao Te Ching* audio book many, many times, and the voice in my head was that of the narrator.

"There are worse plans," I said.

Finding him here made me realize that we were all staying on the right side of the upper compound, which was what Randy Wayne and the others had to expect. Perhaps we'd be safer and have a better chance on the opposite side—behind the Library, Education, PRIDE printing plant, and Food Services, but to get there meant we'd have to cross the road and an open area of some fifty yards where we could be more easily seen.

"If I'm gonna die, it's not gonna be in a cage, but out here under this magic moon."

I nodded, appreciating the sentiment, though I doubted he could see it.

I had been so busy trying to survive and keep us alive, I hadn't taken the time to prepare to die or consider how I wanted to if it came to that.

God grant me the serenity to accept the things I cannot change, the courage to change the things I can, and the wisdom to know the difference.

If I died wasn't ultimately up to me. *How* I died was. *How do I want to die?*

Without fear. At peace. Trying to live, trying to protect Anna and preserve both our lives—but not in a thoughtless, panicked, frenzied way. In a Zen way, doing all I can, then stepping back and accepting what is. I wanted to die on my feet, attempting to do the right thing for the right reasons. I wanted to die honorably. I wanted to be able, though I wasn't sure I could, to have compassion for my killer, to love and forgive with my final breath.

That's what I wanted. What of that I would actually be able to achieve I didn't know, but if I wasn't mindful about it, if I wasn't prayerful and careful, I'd have little chance at all at having a good death.

"Have you seen anyone?" I asked. "Inmates or officers going into and out of buildings? Anything you can tell us?"

"Inmate went into Laundry a little while ago."

I turned and looked toward the laundry building. Through the fog and darkness I could see a faint light coming from a few of the small widows.

"Looked like the one they call the Gainesville Grim Reaper. What's his name? Cantor? He had a weapon too. Looked like the biggest fuckin' carvin' knife you ever seen."

"There's no way you could've seen all that from out here," I said.

"I was closer earlier. Saw him when I was. He went in the chapel for a while. That's when I moved out here. Saw him go in Laundry just a little while ago."

"Okay," I said. "Thanks. You wanna go with us? Fare better if we work together."

"Think I'll stay here. If you figure something out for us or need me, this is where I'll be."

Chapter Forty-five

"Where're we headed?" Anna asked.

"Laundry."

"Seriously? Like some run-toward-the-roar face-your-fears shit?"

I laughed. "Not exactly, no. Well, maybe a little. But more to be unexpected. Switch things up some. Go on the offensive instead of staying on the defensive. How're you feeling?"

"Not so good. But it has less to do with the cuts in my feet and the bleeding coming from my belly than the fact that we're running toward a psychotic serial killer."

She had not seen what Cantor had done to Emmitt, nor had I told her in any detail. If I had or if she had seen it, the fear and dread and nausea she felt now would pale to the point of nonexistence.

"I'm sure it'd be easy to talk me out of," I said.

"I doubt that."

"It may be the worst idea I've ever had," I said, "but it just seemed like Cardigan is lying over there waiting to die. I don't want to do that. I can't."

"I'm glad. I just—"

Just then we were tackled from the side, taken to the ground with force, Anna letting out a painful shriek.

I dropped the bat and it rolled too far away to reach.

I grabbed for Anna, but was on the ground with someone on top of me before I could make any contact at all.

I struggled with the figure on top of me, but only for a moment—only until his partner, who was still straddling Anna, reached over and pressed the barrel of his small handgun to my head.

"See this," he said, tapping me with it, "this will now be pointed at her head. Resist some more if you want to be single for a little while before you die."

I went perfectly still.

They were the two officers from the chapel.

The one on me pushed himself off and told me to stand slowly as the other helped Anna to her feet.

The two men looked vaguely familiar. I had seen them at the prison before, but didn't know their names and probably had never shared more than a passing greeting with them. Certainly not an entire conversation.

The one who had been on top of me was smaller and younger, but both men looked to be in their thirties.

"You okay?" I asked Anna.

"I landed on the baby. It was hard. I don't feel right."

"Real soon all three of you won't feel a thing," the one with the gun said.

He held the gun close to Anna's head, and he was standing too far away for me to reach. I tried to think of our options, but couldn't come up with any.

"We takin' them to the ripper or callin' for someone to bring him to us?" the smaller guy asked.

"Whatever way the boss wants, but Butler wanted a word with that one before we turn the ripper loose on 'em. Maybe all we have to do is turn them over to him and Pine and let them deal with him."

"You don't want to watch him do it?"

"No I sure as shit do not. Was bad enough seeing what he did to that poor prick in the chapel after the fact. That shit's bad enough to not be able to unsee, but actually seein' him do it . . . Might give me ideas for my old lady."

The smaller guy laughed at that. He did it in such a way as to convey his understanding of why, given his old lady, it would be a temptation.

"Get 'em cuffed," the one with the gun said, "and let's ge—"

Ronnie Cardigan jabbed his shank in the left side of the bigger officer's neck and pulled it out, blood spurting as he did, then did it again.

I lunged for the gun, grabbing it from him as he reached for the gush of blood at his neck.

The smaller officer began to run, but Cardigan kicked at his boot and he tripped and fell.

Before I could say or do anything, Ronnie had jumped on him and was stabbing him in the back, then sides and throat.

I hugged and held Anna, watching Cardigan as I did.

She rubbed her stomach, groaning softly, breathing erratically.

In less than two minutes of jumping on the officer, Cardigan was climbing off.

"You saved our lives," I said. "Thank you."

"This is all so fucked up," he said. "All of it. This whole place. All of this. The whole fucking world."

"I know."

He started wandering away, back the way he had come, both of the men he had attacked bleeding out.

"Stay with us," I said. "We can—"

"I can't. I can't handle any more of this shit."

"We have a gun now," I said. "That changes things, changes everything."

He didn't slow or stop or say anything else, just kept walking away, as if any of this was something that could actually be walked away from.

Chapter Forty-six

We had a gun.

It changed things.

It changed everything.

We were still outmanned. We were still outgunned. We were still facing the enormous machinery of a maximum security prison, a handful of desperate men, and a particularly vicious psychopathic killer. They still had the power. Only now they didn't have all of it.

The gun felt good in my hand.

A pocket pistol designed for self-defense, it was extremely small. A black DoubleTap that held just two .9mm rounds. It wasn't much, but it was enough to make a difference.

I thought about the role guns had played in my life, how many times they had saved me and others, how many times I had vowed never to use one again.

I loathed the way part of our population fetishized guns, the paranoid, mostly powerless people who worshiped at an altar of blued and stainless steel, an altar upon which was the blood of millions of martyrs to a religion they weren't even aware existed.

I thought about the hardened, urban street thug and the easily manipulated rural loner, the intercity gang

member and the backwoods militia member. Each turned
to guns for the same reason—their actual or perceived
powerlessness and the promise of immediate actual and
perceived power a handgun held.

Having this small weapon and its two rounds didn't
tip the balance of power in our direction, but it did give
us a measure of the immediate power those who perceive
themselves to be powerless loved so much about guns. I
would use the weapon to protect Anna, and I was grateful
for it and the ability to do just that, but I couldn't love guns,
couldn't worship them. But because of the work I did, the
life I led, I also hadn't been able to give them up completely
either.

Since I had yet to be able to follow Jesus's teachings
regarding going out into the world unarmed, not resisting
evil, and turning the other cheek when attacked, I did
my best to follow Lao Tzu and remember that *Weapons
are the tools of fear; a decent man will avoid them except in the
direst necessity and, if compelled, will use them only with the utmost
restraint.*

Of course, Jesus's instructions were for facing down
an oppressive empire while Lao Tzu's were for personal
day-to-day application, but I took both seriously, both as
sacred instruction and an ideal I aspired to.

I was in the direst of situations, but only wanted
to use the utmost of restraint, and be nothing less than a
decent man.

"How are you feeling?" I asked Anna.

We were easing our way over toward the laundry
building, slowly, steadily.

"I must be in shock. That was so . . . I feel so
conflicted. I wouldn't wish that on anyone, but I was glad it
happened to them."

"Welcome to my world."

"It is, isn't it? I don't see how you do it, how you handle it so well."

"I don't think I do."

"You absolutely do. It'd be so easy to be at either extreme, but you . . . you're the most gentle man I've ever known, yet you are capable of violence—but always with great restraint."

"Yeah," I said, "you're in shock."

"Does having the gun change our plans any?" she asked.

"It only holds two rounds. It won't be much help. So . . . no. Not really."

"Are you really going to attack Cantor?" she asked. "Will you just shoot him?"

"My goal is to subdue him," I said. "I'd like to take him off the board if I can."

"Promise me you'll shoot him if you have to, that you won't get yourself hurt or killed because you're trying too hard not to kill anyone else."

"Promise."

"Holdin' you to it."

As we neared Laundry, Cantor, carrying his knife, walked out.

We froze.

I now had the bat in one hand, the small gun in the other, and I readied myself.

He headed left, toward Food Services, without ever even looking in our direction.

"You can go up behind him and shoot him in the head," Anna whispered. "Won't get a better opportunity than this."

"I was going to try to knock him out with the bat," I said. "Never intended to shoot him and certainly not in the back."

She nodded without saying anything.

I was really hoping not to shoot anyone—especially in the back. It wasn't something I thought I could do. Of course, I could do it to save Anna, but there was no way to know until it was too late that doing that would save her. If I could be sure it was the only way, I'd do it. I'd do it without hesitation and with no regret—like breaking Cardigan out to trade for her. But could I do it without knowing I had to? Could I do it just on the chance it would save her?

And it wasn't just the issue of back-shooting a man, a psychopathic killer, but it was the consideration that it would alert the others to our whereabouts—particularly if I did it out in the open where he was now. It would use one or both of our only rounds and take away the surprise element of us having a weapon.

But it was mostly not wanting to back-shoot a man in cold blood.

"So what now?" she asked.

"Looks like he left the door open," I said. "We go in, charge the phone, and use it."

"Okay."

"You think I should go shoot Cantor in the back of the head, don't you?" I said.

"I just hope you don't regret not doing it later."

Chapter Forty-seven

Confirming Cantor had left the door to Laundry open, we ducked inside and closed it.

To our left were enormous industrial, round, stainless steel washing machines, a complex series of large white PVC pipes running into and out of them from above and behind. On the back wall was a bank of huge battleship-gray industrial dryers. On the right side of the room were pressing machines and large folding tables. In front of, in between, and around everything were some fifty rolling canvas laundry carts on wood frames and casters filled with inmate uniforms, bedding, blankets, and towels.

"Before we do anything else, I'd like you to lie down on some of these blankets," I said. "We could hide you in the back behind the dryers or even inside one of the carts beneath some laundry. So no matter what happens next, you'll be able keep your feet up and take pressure off the baby."

"I don't want to be alone."

"As in you don't want me to leave the building or don't even want me across the room?"

"Don't want you leaving the building."

"Okay."

"Had you planned to?" she asked.

"I thought I might look around a little while you rested."

"'Cause you can move quicker and be more stealthy without a pregnant woman in tow?"

"You're very stealthy," I said. "I just—doesn't matter. I'm not going anywhere. Let's plug in the phone and get you situated."

Which was what we did next, piling blankets in the back corner behind a row of carts and beneath a folding table and easing her onto them. Her feet up and phone plugged in beside her, I left her there to rest while I began to look around the building.

I had only taken a few steps when the power went off.

A couple of dim emergency backup lights flickered on.

"Shit," Anna said.

"They must be cutting it off building by building after they've been searched."

"That or they know we're in here," she said.

I was already making my way toward the door to take a look outside, but her comment made me wonder if instead I should go help her up and get her out of here.

I hesitated for a moment, trying to decide what to do, then continued to the door and looked out.

Pine Tree was rounding the backside of the medical building and heading this way.

Think. Get out or prepare to fight. Back door. Get Anna. Get out.

There was a back door in the building. I'd grab Anna and we'd leave through it.

"Come on, baby," I said. "We've got to go. Don't bump your head getting up. Ease up and we'll sneak out the back door. Pine Tree Peavey is heading over here."

She didn't respond.

Surely she hadn't fallen asleep that quickly. She could have, as exhausted as she was.

"Anna?"

Still no response.

Had she passed out from all the blood she had lost?

When I reached the spot where I had left her, she wasn't there.

"Anna?"

The phone was there. The blankets were. She was not.

I looked around the dim room, searching for her in every direction.

"Anna?" I said, starting to panic. "Anna?"

She wasn't there.

If she could answer, she would. Did someone have her? Were they still in the building or had they dragged her out the back door? Would they kill her instantly or keep her alive long enough to use her for leverage? If Cantor had her it would be the former. If the officers, perhaps the latter.

I began moving through the building, looking behind and beneath and around its many objects and obstacles, knowing that at any moment, Pine would be coming through the front door.

"Anna?"

I ran over to the back door and looked out into the dark, crimson-tinged night.

There was no sign of her. No sign of anyone.

Not sure what I should do next, but knowing I had to deal with the immediate threat of Pine, I raced back across the building with the bat.

Standing on the side the door opened into, I pulled

the bat back and waited.

When he opened the door, he just stood there in the doorway, scanning the room, the door between us blocking him from me and the bat.

But when he stepped in and let the door close, I swung as hard as I could.

Because he was so tall, the blow got him mostly on the back and only a little on his head.

If it did anything but get his attention I couldn't tell.

As he turned toward me, I tried to swing again, but he caught the bat with both hands and jerked it away from me.

Quickly flipping it around to get a better grip, he handled it like someone familiar, comfortable, a former high school baseball star.

The bat looked small in his hands, as if a child's instead of the full-size it was.

I began backing away, trying to figure out what to do, backing into and around one of the folding tables and knocking off a pile of blankets as I did.

He came after me.

Lumbering steadily but unhurriedly toward me like a predator knowing its prey is trapped, he slowly, confidently kept coming.

"Pine," Randy Wayne said on the radio on Pine's belt. "You got him?"

"Got him," Pine said into the mic clipped to his shoulder.

"Scott, you got the girl?"

"Got 'er."

"Where?" I asked Pine. "Where does he have her? How'd he—"

"Butler, get Cantor over there and let's finish this."

Circling the folding table, I kept it between us. Pine,

frustrated and out of breath, continued laboring around after me.

"Why're you doin' this?" I asked. "How can you be okay with killin' us in cold blood?"

He didn't respond.

"Where does Branson have Anna?"

Without breaking his stride, he slammed into the table and drove it into me, both dropping me and knocking the breath out of me.

As I fell, I struck my head on the metal corner of one of the pressing machines.

Jarred. Dizzy. Head throbbing instantly. Gasping to get a breath.

Pine was making his way toward me, slinging the large table out of his way with one hand.

I tried to roll, to climb to my feet, but my body wouldn't cooperate.

With all the strength I could muster, with all the effort I could give, I was only able to get to my hands and knees.

Shoving myself up so I was hunched back on my knees, I freed my hands up and plunged them into my pockets.

When Pine reached me, he snatched me upright, holding me in front of him as if I were a child.

I found the small can of Fredericka's hairspray, brought it up with my left hand, and sprayed it in his face.

It was no more than a minor annoyance but he released me to wipe it out of his eyes.

As he did, I removed the lighter from my right pocket and lit it.

Holding the small flame in front of his face, I sprayed the hairspray again.

It burned his face. His hair and the top of his shirt caught on fire and I sprayed some more.

He shrieked and began patting out his hair and shirt, dropping the bat as he did.

Bending down and grabbing the bat, I brought it up into his chin like an uppercut. He staggered back, still stamping out the fire.

I swung the bat again, this time at his enormous midsection. The blow was hard and landed well, doubling him over.

With him lowered now, I swung at the back of his head, a cracking hit that felled him.

On his hands and knees now, I hit him again, another hard shot to the back of the head.

This time he went all the way down and didn't move.

I stamped out the last of the flames on his shirt, took his radio, and ran to look for Anna.

Chapter Forty-eight

As I searched the laundry building for Anna again, I turned up the volume on Pine's radio just enough for me to hear and pressed it against my ear.

Butler was saying, "I can't find him."

"Scott, what about you?" Randy Wayne said.

"Negatory."

"Chase? Dale? What about y'all?"

No response.

"Pine? Did he come back there?"

"Ain't here," I said, trying to sound like Pine.

"Chase? Dale? Y'all there? Over?"

"Fuck," Butler said. "You think Cantor got them too?"

As they continued to talk and I steadily searched the building, I began to devise a plan that might both create a distraction and get us some help.

"I'll get Cantor," Randy Wayne said. "Y'all just get them to the chapel. And hurry. We're runnin' out of time."

"Ten-four," Butler said.

"Pine, you got Jordan and Cardigan or just—"

"Just the chaplain," I said. "Ain't seen Cardigan."

"Anybody seen him?"

No one responded.

"Even better," he said. "We'll send in the response team to take him out as soon as we finish with his victims. Hurry everybody. IG's about fifteen minutes out. Let's finish this shit and give her a good show when she gets here."

Grabbing as many towels and sheets and T-shirts as I could find, I piled them into one of the canvas carts and rolled it into the back right corner beneath the gas heater hanging from the ceiling.

There were thousands of blankets stacked against the walls in the back corner, but my guess was they had been made of flame retardant material.

Sliding one of the folding tables against the closest dryer, I jumped up on it, clutching a sheet in my hand as I did. I then climbed up on top of the dryer. Confirming the pilot was lit, I draped the sheet around the heater, letting it hang down to the cart below.

Climbing back down, I used the hairspray and lighter to set the cheap cotton clothes in the cart on fire.

Before they even reached the hanging sheet, the pilot from the heater had already lit the top part and flames were beginning to run down.

As the fire grew, I rolled other carts with clothes in them over and began lighting them.

The fire continued to grow and spread.

As I ran over toward Pine, gas from the heater began to feed the flame and with a giant *whoooosh* it shot flames out, lighting other clothing and carts.

When I reached Pine, he was beginning to stir a little.

I slapped him hard across the face, trying to avoid his burns.

"Fire," I said. "You need to crawl out of here. Now."

He moved his head and moaned a little, but that was

all.

I slapped him hard again, and again got the same response.

Leaning down and grabbing his arms, I began to drag him toward the front door.

It was very slow going, and I wasn't sure how much longer I could do it.

Smoke was beginning to fill the building and it was hard to breathe.

About halfway to the door, he looked up at me drowsily, coughed, and said, "What . . . What . . . are . . . you . . . doin'?"

"Fire," I said. "Got to get you out of here. Can you help? Can you crawl or walk or—"

"Yeah. I got it. I can get it from here."

"You sure?" I asked, releasing his arms.

He nodded and began to crawl toward the door.

As he did, as a fire alarm began to sound in the quiet night, I ran out the back door, back out into the night, back beneath the beginning-to-wan blood moon in search of the girl I had been in love with since we were children.

Chapter Forty-nine

"What the fuck is that?" Randy Wayne yelled into the radio.

If the timing had worked out the way I hoped, he was out of the control room and on the compound with us. His question indicated that he was.

"Fire alarm," Butler said.

"No shit. Where?"

"Don't know."

"Scotty?"

"No idea."

"Pine?"

I was running as fast as I could toward the chapel, scanning the area around and in front of me for movement.

"Pine?"

I didn't respond. Kept moving.

Lights on the compound began to flicker on and in the distance a fire whistle whined in the unnaturally quiet night.

"Firefighters and emergency response will be here soon," Randy Wayne said. "We have even less time than we thought."

As I reached the chapel, I could see Anna through

the back windows.

To my surprise, she was being held by Randy Wayne himself.

The back door was propped open. Without slowing I went inside.

Anna was cuffed and barely conscious, held up by Randy Wayne just a few feet in front of where Emmitt was nailed to the podium. Branson and Butler stood nearby.

Anna, who must have been drugged, was finding it difficult to stand.

"We're running out of time," Randy Wayne said into the radio he was holding. "Hurry to the chapel, John."

He then tossed the radio to Branson.

The chapel was eerily lit, its darkness streaked with carmine-colored light from the moon, three emergency backup lights, one of which was below Emmitt and cast wicked shadows on the ceiling and back wall, and some weak, random illumination spilling in from the front where now lamps were blinking on.

"Yep," Randy Wayne said when he saw me. "All that was for your benefit. Well, not all of it, but a lot. Okay, some. I appreciate you obliging and rushing on up here for us. The fire alarm your work?"

I nodded.

"How about Chase and Dale and Pine not joining us?"

I shrugged.

"Surrender your weapon," he said, wrapping the hand that had been holding the radio around Anna's throat.

I looked down at the bat. I had forgotten I had it.

Butler stepped over and took it from me.

Gripping it by the wrong end, he then slung it around and tagged me on the side of the neck with it. The blow was hard but glancing.

I took a step toward him.

"NO," Randy Wayne said, and he punched Anna hard in the stomach.

Anna gasped and began to cry.

I stopped. "Okay. Just don't do that again."

"What?" he asked. "This?" And did it again. "That's for making us chase your ass all night. Now, while we wait for Cantor to get here, if we hit you, you turn the other cheek. Got it?"

I nodded.

"Here, come hold this fat bitch up," he said. "I'm too tired to deal with this shit."

I rushed over to Anna and wrapped my arms around her.

"I wish you two didn't have to die tonight," he said. "I truly and sincerely do. But . . . come on . . . since you do, isn't it nice to be in each other's arms? Life's little consolation. Am I right? Gotta be grateful for the small stuff. Between you and me . . . that's all there is."

The front door to the chapel opened and they all turned to see who was coming in.

"I love you," I said to Anna. "I'm so sorry about all this."

"I think I'm losing the baby," she said. "I'm so scared."

Pine walked through the doors and up the center aisle toward us.

"Just come when you can, big fella," Randy Wayne said. "What's burning?"

When he got closer, his missing hair, charred shirt, and the burns on his face and neck could be seen.

"Besides *you*," Randy Wayne said. "Shit. What the fuck happened?"

"Laundry was burnin'. 'Bout out by now. Chaplain got me when we were fighting."

"*He* did that to you?"

"What's goin' on here?"

"Just waitin' for Cantor to haul his big knife up here."

"Then what? Stand around and watch as he does that to them?" he asked, nodding at Emmitt.

"I hope he won't just repeat what he's already done," Randy Wayne said. "He's far more creative than that. Although . . . if he did . . . he could do the two thieves crucified with Jesus. That could be interesting. Who do you think he'd choose for Christ, though? The chaplain's the obvious choice, but I'd be disappointed if he went with something so on the nose. Wouldn't you?"

Pine began shaking his head. "I can't just stand here and let that sick psycho carve them up. Thought I could, but I can't."

"No problem. Go back outside and keep an eye on things. We'll be out in a—"

"No, I mean I can't stand by and let it happen."

"Come again?"

"I just can't. Chaplain could've let me burn in that building down there. He didn't. I can't let that go un—"

"Pine, he burned your fuckin' face and half your hair off. The fuck you mean you can't do it?"

"He could've let me die. He didn't."

I had seen the power of mercy change people before, but never as immediately as this. It wasn't why I did it, but as unintended consequences go, it wasn't a bad one. Of course, Pine was probably having doubts about what they were doing already. Me helping him out of the burning building may have had nothing to do with it.

"Two choices, Pine. Both involve them dying. Only

one involves you dying with them."

"Can't let you kill them."

"You'll lose your job," Randy Wayne said. "Be arrested. Go to prison."

"Look at that," Pine said, nodding toward Emmitt. "You can stand by or worse watch while he does that to them?"

"I wish it didn't have to be this way, but we got no other choices now—especially now. We're too far in. It's way too late to . . . The point of no return was way the fuck back there."

Pine looked over at Branson and Butler. "Come on guys. Think about this. You can't be okay with this."

"What we're not okay with is the alternative," Branson said.

Pine shook his swollen and burned head and began laboring toward us.

"Y'all are gonna have to kill me too," he said.

"No problem," Randy Wayne said. Then turning to Branson and Butler added, "Finish him off."

"With what?" Butler asked. "We got no weapons."

"You've got a fuckin' baseball bat," he said. "Worked pretty well on you."

"I got this," Branson said.

He stepped over and prepared to attack Pine.

"Help him," Randy Wayne said to Butler.

Butler halfheartedly followed Branson a little way down the center aisle, staying several steps behind him.

Pine crouched in a defensive stance, his arms up, ready to take the bat away from Branson in the same way he had me.

As Branson charged him, Cantor came out from behind the podium, striking me on the back of the neck with the handle of his huge knife.

My knees buckled and as I was falling he kicked me. I flew across the front of the chapel and went down hard.

Without me to hold her up, Anna collapsed.

Cantor pounced on her. Straddling her, actually sitting on her pregnant belly and bouncing.

Anna shrieked, then screamed, then began to cry.

"Sneaky son of a gun," Randy Wayne exclaimed. "He was hiding back there this whole time."

His attention was divided between what Cantor was doing to Anna and the fight between Pine and his boys.

I was flat on the floor, belly crawling like a baby toward Anna. I wasn't very far away, but wouldn't make it in time.

Cantor began cutting her clothes and peeling them off her in strips.

"Lovely," he said. "So very lovely."

She was crying and ineffectually struggling against the horror of what was happening to her.

"She *is* a good-looking woman under there, ain't she?" Randy Wayne said. "Show us some more before you start to make a mess of her. I wanna see that pristine pussy."

Cantor continued working as if Randy Wayne hadn't spoken.

Between her gasps and breathy cries, Anna breathed my name. "John."

I thought about all the different ways she had said my name over the years—the nuances and shadings and all the tiny variations. I loved the sound of my name in her mouth—especially lately when, for the first time in our lifetime of loving one another, it had been said in intense and intimate ecstasy.

I still couldn't get my feet and legs to work. The best

I could do was crawl across the carpet.

I continued to crawl.

I didn't want the final time Anna said my name to be in pain, spoken during the terror of violation, humiliation, and degradation. I didn't want to spend the rest of my life, no matter how long or short it might be, haunted by the sound of my name said as a plea for help I was unable to give.

Pine was putting up a good fight, giving it an impressive and valiant effort, but then Branson struck him in the back of the knees with the bat and he went down.

Both men began to whale on him then, Butler kicking and stomping with his boots, Branson working the bat.

Cantor had Anna's shirt open, and with one flick of his blade he sprung her bra loose.

Her beautiful, bare breasts being exposed like that, Cantor and Randy Wayne gawking at them, made her look even more vulnerable than she had before.

My extremities began to tingle.

"Don't cut her yet," Randy Wayne was saying. "More. Show me more."

Though being brutally beaten, Pine continued to crawl toward Cantor in a manner not dissimilar to the way I was crawling toward Anna.

"Let's see her sweet little snatch," Randy Wayne was saying. "Come on."

As Cantor readjusted himself, I lunged toward him, but was too weak and too far away, and fell short.

"Finish him off first so we can take a little more time with her."

As if following orders, which I knew he wasn't, Cantor stood and walked over to me.

Squatting down to straddle me the way he had been

Anna a moment before, he rolled me over.

As he did, I reached into my pocket and brought out the small DoubleTap.

Raising the knife above his head and preparing to thrust it into my heart, he slung his head back and shuddered a little in exhilaration.

That's when I reached up, pressed the small gun into the bottom of his chin, and pulled the trigger.

He dropped the knife and collapsed on top of me.

"Where the fuck did he get a gun?" Randy Wayne said.

I bucked and rolled and squirmed Cantor off as Randy Wayne rushed me.

As he ran past Anna, she kicked her leg out and tripped him.

He fell within a few feet of me and reached for Cantor's knife.

With Cantor still partially on me, I couldn't move— not in time.

What do I do? Think. Not many options. One chance. Once choice. One bullet. Make it count.

I brought the gun down beside my leg and shot Randy Wayne in the face.

With their attention diverted onto us, Branson and Butler didn't realize Pine was rising behind them.

It was something they would only ever know for the briefest of brutal moments.

Grabbing their heads with his giant bloody paws, he slammed them together, snapping their necks and crushing their skulls, collapsing alongside them when he was done.

Chapter Fifty

Anna was rushed to the hospital.

Rachel Peterson arrived and began to clean up the mess and conduct the investigation. Her first comment to me was "Y'all really take the blood moon literally around here, don't you?"

My chapel was a gruesome crime scene.

The entire upper compound of PCI was processed for evidence.

The fire department arrived and put out the fire in Laundry.

Pine and Randy Wayne, who was in critical condition but not dead, were taken into custody and to different hospitals.

Ronnie Cardigan, who was right where he had been when I tripped over him earlier in the night, was placed in protective custody, then transferred to another institution.

After the various crime scenes were processed, Cantor, Chase, Dale, Branson, Butler, and Emmitt were transported to the morgue by the same funeral home that had recently lost the body of another murder victim found at the prison.

Marty Perkins, Lewis Milner, and Jack Kirkus were arrested in connection with the death of Reggie Dalton.

Over the next few days, Rachel interviewed me, Cardigan, Anna, and Pine.

Pine was particularly helpful and would receive consideration for being so—and for attempting to help me and Anna in the end. There were many holes he couldn't fill in. Randy Wayne, who was still in a coma and probably wouldn't make it, was the only one who could provide this missing information—something he most likely wouldn't do even if he were conscious.

Three days had passed.

I was about to head back to the hospital after a quick shower when Rachel Peterson pulled into my front yard.

"How's she doing?" Rachel asked.

"Little better each day," I said.

"I know you're in a hurry, but before I head back to Central Office, I wanted to have one more quick chat."

I nodded.

I had actually been getting in the car when she pulled up, but wanted to hear what she had to say.

I walked over and we both leaned on her state-issued car, the empty, open Prairie Palm stretching out before us.

She was dressed the way she had been when we first met—in jeans, boots, and a button-down. Her hair was pulled back in a ponytail revealing the darkish skin of her face and neck. Her ID and badge were clipped to her belt, hanging down above her left leg.

"Never said how impressive what you did was," she said. "Surviving what you did is one thing. Doing it with a pregnant woman is another."

"Could've very easily gone the other way," I said.

"Came way too close a couple of times. Without Cardigan and Pine . . ."

"They helped themselves plenty by helpin' you," she said. "Whatta you think about Cardigan's story?"

"Did you find the other camera?"

She nodded. "Like not to have. Shit was hidden like a mofo. Long since recorded over whatever was on it. No help at all."

"Still might be," I said.

"It's no wonder he didn't mention it until he thought he was gonna die," she said.

"Why's that?"

"We found two."

"Yeah?"

"The other was set up in the victim's bedroom. He was Peeping Tom her in high def, creepy little fucker. Probably why he didn't mention it as part of his defense— that or he really killed her."

"If he had been tried for her murder, he would've been forced to reveal them, but since he was only facing drug and burglary charges . . ."

"Or he killed her and the footage wouldn't help," she said.

"Or that."

"What did you mean, it still might be helpful?"

"If Cardigan's not the killer," I said. "Did you find any connections to Tom Daniels?"

She nodded. "Actually, I did. Not to Cardigan, Reggie Dalton, or any of the officers involved, but to the victim, Ashley Fountain. Phone records show calls between them. That's all I got so far, but . . ."

I thought about it. "Could've been using again, getting his drugs from her. Could've been using her other services if she was working as a prostitute. Maybe both."

"Probably both. We're still going through her phone records. She was a very popular girl."

"Find out anything else about the actor?" I asked.

"Not really. He's been in rehab a few times. Popped for possession twice. So had two strikes, but nothin' in his background makes sense for him doing a kidnapping. And about that . . . I've thought a lot about it. Nobody's gonna find out about the little field trip you took Ronnie Cardigan on."

"Really?" I asked, genuinely surprised.

Her bright, gray-green eyes locked onto mine and she held my gaze.

"But I'm the reason Emerson is dead," I said.

"Actually, it's a knife-happy serial killer Randy Wayne Davis let out of Closed Custody and loose on the compound."

"You know what I mean."

"And you know what *I* mean."

"Did you find out why Randy Wayne and the others were doing all this for Perkins, Milner, and Kirkus?" I asked.

"They're all part of the same corrupt little house of cards. If those three went down, the rest of 'em would. They had all kinds of rackets and schemes going. There are a few others we haven't gotten yet, but we will. It's funny, even with all Pine has done, he's hesitant to give up the others. The department issued a statement that the officers involved are a very small minority and are no reflection on the fine men and women who do a difficult job honorably day in and day out. It's true, but . . ."

I nodded. "Absolute power corrupts absolutely," I said. "We work in an institution where one group has all the power over another."

We were quiet a moment.

In our silence other sounds could be heard. The Apalachicola River swirling its way toward the bay behind us. The desultory sounds drifting over from Phase I of the Prairie Palm, the one that was actually inhabited. They came to us from across the field and on the other side of a stand of pines to our left. A door slamming. A dog barking. The shrieks and yells of kids playing. Pop music played too loudly, distorted yet muted by the distance and objects between us.

Eventually she said, "What's bothering you, John?"

"My conscience, among other things," I said.

"Emmitt Emerson?"

I nodded.

"Let's talk about the other things," she said. "What's bothering you about the case?"

"There's something we're not seeing," I said. "There's more going on here."

"Like what?"

I shrugged. "I don't know. I can't see it all yet."

"Tell me the parts you can see—or at least what you think about them."

"Why go to all the trouble of blackmailing me to break Cardigan out? They could've killed him inside. They could've had Cantor do it. And if they wanted it away from the prison, away from them, why get me to do it? They could've faked an escape and killed him in the woods or a hundred miles away."

She seemed to think about it.

"There are other things," I said. "I don't know. I've got to go. Don't want to be away from Anna any longer."

"Okay, but let's talk about those other things soon. Think of anything in the meantime, call me."

Chapter Fifty-one

Anna was in Bay Medical Center, the same hospital as Chris, and when I arrived he was in her room with their new baby girl, Taylor Elizabeth Taunton.

Anna had undergone an emergency C-section because of the trauma she and little Taylor had endured, but both mother and child were fine, healthy, happy.

Chris was beside Anna's bed in a wheelchair, Taylor cradled in his arms fast asleep.

"Hey," Anna said when I walked in, her face lighting up.

Her welcome was warm and sincerely enthusiastic, and made me feel a little less like an intruder, a little less like an interloper interrupting a family moment. For whatever else they were, they were a family.

Chris nodded in a not completely unwelcoming way.

I walked to the other side of the bed and sat in the bulky wooden-framed, fake-leather chair there.

"How are the patients?" I asked.

"Better now," Anna said. "So glad you're back. Beth is good. Had a good feeding and has been out hard ever since."

"Beth?" I said.

"Trying it on. Whatta you think?"

"I like it."

"I like Taylor best," Chris said, "but I don't dislike Beth."

"And Beth's mom?" I said. "How is she?"

"Sore. Sleepy. Traumatized."

I took her hand in mine.

Being in the sterile, spartan room made me anxious to get my girls home, but when I thought of my home, of the small rundown trailer that should've been condemned long before I ever moved into it, I realized I could never take them there.

"Chris?" I asked.

"Get to go home today."

"That's good."

Where can we live? What can I find for us before Anna and Beth are released?

"I just wanted to stop by, see my girls, and say something," he said. "You saved my daughter's life. I'll never forget that. Anna's too. That means more to me than you'll ever know. Now, I intend to win Anna back, to save my marriage and have my family back together."

"It's too late for that," Anna said.

"But until I do, I just wanted you to know that I appreciate what you did, and I won't be causing you any trouble. I'm a changed man. Was before, but now, with little Taylor here . . . I've been born again."

I thought of what Frederick Buechner had written. *When a child is born, a father is born.*

He started to hand Beth back to Anna, but winced, and realizing Anna couldn't twist down or lift her, said, "Could you . . ."

I was already walking around the bed to help.

I carefully took her from him, cradled and kissed her,

and gave her to her mother. I then returned to my chair.

The door was slightly ajar and from the hallway
the sounds of the hospital could be heard—a code being
announced, a doctor being paged, some electronic beeps
and mechanical laboring, and competing TVs turned up
entirely too loud.

"Is it really too late?" he asked. "I thought it never
was. Isn't that what you teach, John? Doesn't Taylor need
her daddy? Wouldn't it be better for her, for all of us, if we
were a family?"

"You helped save us," Anna said. "Literally saved
Merrill's life. I'm so grateful to you for that. And you will
always be Taylor's dad, and I hope you have changed and
will be a good father to her. But I want to be clear about
this. I don't want any misunderstanding or room for false
hope. You and I are done. We have been for a long time.
I'm with John and will be until I draw my final breath. I'm
not trying to be cruel, just clear."

"But I have changed. And I did save your life—a
couple of times."

"Did you?" I said.

"What?"

"I was just wondering if you really did."

"Whatta you mean?"

I took a breath, trying to decide if I was really about
to do what I seemed to have already begun.

"Here's an alternative theory. You were behind
it in the first place—in on it with Randy Wayne. Anna
sensed three different kidnappers at different times. One
wouldn't come close to her, wouldn't say anything. That
was you. You couldn't get close or say a word without her
recognizing you. She knows you too well, is too familiar
with everything about you."

"What the fuck? Are you out of your—"

"In the hospital when you were talking about the kidnappers, you mentioned two guys, not three. That's because you were the third. You didn't count yourself."

"Do you have any idea how absurd you sound?"

"As an attorney you come across a lot of desperate, compromised, and criminal people," I said. "Like corrupt correctional officers, drug-addicted actors, and students arrested for theft and possession who know a lot about security systems. I keep asking myself, how did you happen to show up at just the right moment at our house? How did you act so heroically?"

"They shot me, for fuck's sake," he said.

"Exactly," I said. "Didn't kill you like they said they did. Sure, you were shot, but it wasn't nearly as bad as you pretended it was. You set all this up and made Anna your witness. She didn't see any of what happened. Just heard it. And while we're on her, she said she couldn't've been cared for any better. Seems a little strange. The person doing all the talking, the one who sometimes sounds like he's reading and who calls her my wife to further deflect suspicion off of you, is just an actor playing a part."

"You sick son of a bitch," Anna said, pulling Taylor more closely to her, holding her more protectively.

"This is nuts. This is . . . Why would I do any of this?"

"You did it the *way* you did it to take me and Cardigan out and get Anna back. I kept wondering why the elaborate scheme to get me involved and get Cardigan outside the institution. That's why."

"You think I did all this just to get Anna back? That's—"

"No, I said the *way* you did it was to get rid of us and win her back. The reason you did it was far more sinister. You and the others had to take Cardigan out."

"*Me?* I have nothing to do with—"

"You were sleeping with Ashley Fountain. Buying drugs from her. She was pregnant. Was it your child? Was she planning to tell Anna? Report you to the Florida Bar? They're still going through her phone records. I bet they find calls between the two of you. Lots of them. You killed her, made it look like suicide, and framed Ronnie for stealing from her, bringing him under suspicion for her death."

This was all conjecture and guesswork, of course, but it fit and since I had come this far, I was going all-in, shoving my entire pile of chips to the center of the table.

"I don't know if you knew before then that he had such an elaborate surveillance system or found out when you broke in," I said, "but my guess is you already knew. So when Randy Wayne or Kirkus or whoever you represent— something that won't be hard to determine—called you about what they had done to Reggie Dalton, you told them exactly who could help with the surveillance system."

"Do you know how many clients I've represented over the years?" Chris said. "So what if a couple of COs from PCI are my clients."

"You made sure your partner represented Ronnie," I said. "You couldn't do it yourself, but you wanted to stay close to the case, keep an eye on things. The case against Ronnie was weak, but you made sure he got sent away."

"Upton helped you with this?" Anna said.

"No," Chris said. "There is no *this*. *This* is insane. This is a CO making up shit to try to cut a deal. No one will believe any of this. There's no evidence to support any of this ludicrous bullshit."

"Actually," I said, "Cardigan had two cameras far more hidden than the others. One was in Ashley's bedroom. One was in the closet where his system was so he could see who stole it. You're on both. The one in her bedroom shows you not only sleeping with and doing drugs with her but giving her gifts—gifts that can be traced to you."

He looked at Anna. "You know I cheated. I've sworn to you that I'll never do it again. I didn't kill her. I didn't set up anyone. I took the cameras because I didn't want you to ever have to see any of that. I was so ashamed. So guilty. I felt so bad. I'm so sorry. You have to believe me. You know me. You know I couldn't kill anyone."

"Like the actor? What was his . . . Karl Jason?"

"That was . . . He was . . ."

"There's no way that kid was going to shoot Merrill. You told him to pretend to so you could kill him. Eliminate a witness. Make yourself look heroic. It's premeditated murder."

"Get the fuck out of here," Anna said. "And stay the fuck away from us. Now you don't just need a divorce but a criminal attorney. And I hope they're both the most incompetent, overcharging charlatans on the planet. After you, of course."

Chapter Fifty-two

"Tell me again how you got him to confess all that," Rachel Peterson said.

It was two days later.

We were standing outside the duplex once shared by Ronnie Cardigan and Ashley Fountain. Inside, the FDLE crime scene unit was taking the place apart—literally, forensically.

Chris was in custody. He had been offered a plea deal if he'd testify against Randy Wayne and the others, but in case he didn't, in case, instead of confessing, he decided to claim his innocence and demand to see the evidence against him I had mostly made up, FDLE, TDP, and Rachel's office were not only processing Ronnie and Ashley's duplex, but going through his old phone and bank records and interviewing Anna to see what help she might be able to provide.

"I mean, you had nothing, right?" she said.

"Didn't have much."

"You had nothing."

"I had enough," I said.

"Yeah, to hum a few bars and fake the rest."

"Sometimes that's all you got."

"How much did you make up?"

"More than a little. If he hadn't believed we had him on camera . . ."

"If he hadn't been guilty," she said. "If you hadn't been right."

"I thought he might believe Cardigan was good enough and paranoid enough to have more cameras than he'd found. I knew if he had seen himself on the footage captured by the ones he took, he would actually picture himself on the others. I made up him giving her gifts, but I figured a guy like him was the type to give shiny trinkets to buy, bribe, and impress a young girl like Ashley."

"Did you know you were going to do it when I stopped by your place?"

I shook my head. "Didn't know I was going to do anything until the moment I did. Some of the pieces began to come together on my drive over to the hospital, but I planned to check more of it out before I said or did anything."

"And call me."

"And call you, of course."

"That whole checking more of it out thing would've been a good idea," she said.

I nodded. "It was an impulsive, amateurish mistake," I said, "which may have had something to do with him being . . . who he is."

"Anna's ex."

"Yeah, that."

"Can't remember the last time anyone surprised or impressed me," she said. "You've done both this week. Twice. I look forward to doin' some blood work with you John Jordan. I really do."

After leaving the crime scene, I drove around the neighborhood for a few minutes, trying to prepare myself to face Tom and Sarah Daniels—and Susan if she happened to be there, though I suspected she had long since moved back to Atlanta.

I hadn't liked the way things had ended between us, and had been trying to get in touch for a very long time. After speaking with Tom by phone earlier in the week, I had been curious to know what he thought I had figured out, what he thought I knew that he didn't want me knowing.

Was it connected to his calls to Ashley or something else entirely?

I had to know. I couldn't get this close to his home and not stop in and look into his eyes.

I probably shouldn't. I should probably be glad the entire family is out of my life. I should probably just let all that had happened—and them along with it—go, but I couldn't. Something deep inside was compelling me to knock on his door and see what happened.

I wasn't ready. I wasn't going to be. But I was as ready as I was going to get anytime soon—maybe ever.

I didn't pull into the driveway, instead parked on the street several car lengths down from their house.

I walked toward the familiar dwelling, feeling old familiar feelings. Susan and I had made love in this house. Tom and I had discussed cases in this house. I had witnessed Sarah's PTSD in this house. We had crashed here after FSU football games and concerts and DOC meetings. One of Susan's too-many bridal showers had been here. So had our engagement party cookout. This house was haunted for me.

Mind racing, heart pounding, I walked up the drive, along the stone path, and onto the front stoop.

Standing in front of the enormous oak door, I took a breath and let it out slowly.

I hadn't seen any of these people who were once family since I had accused Tom of murder and Susan had said if I turned him in she'd not only end us, but the life of our child just beginning to grow inside her.

This would not go well. It would not end in any way pretty, only in pain. But I couldn't not knock.

So I did.

To my surprise, it wasn't Tom or Sarah, but Susan who opened the door. To my shock, she was holding a small child who could only be our daughter.

She had been distracted, looking back over her shoulder, opening the door like someone expecting takeout delivery.

It took her a moment to realize what was happening, not just that she was seeing me, but that I was seeing the beautiful, brown-eyed creature she was holding.

With recognition and realization came an extreme mix of emotion, culminating in tears—tears that streamed not poured, tears she wiped away with her free hand.

Something inside Susan broke. I could see it happening.

It took her a moment before she could speak, but when she did . . . she managed to say some of the sweetest words I'd ever heard, as if her carrying and giving birth to our baby had been truly transformative, as if in this moment, that we shared a daughter was all that mattered.

"John, I'd like you to meet Johanna. Johanna, this is your daddy."

About the Author

Multi-award-winning novelist Michael Lister is a native Floridian best known for literary suspense thrillers and mysteries.

The Florida Book Review says that "Vintage Michael Lister is poetic prose, exquisitely set scenes, characters who are damaged and faulty," and Michael Koryta says, "If you like crime writing with depth, suspense, and sterling prose, you should be reading Michael Lister," while Publisher's Weekly adds, "Lister's hard-edged prose ranks with the best of contemporary noir fiction."

Michael grew up in North Florida near the Gulf of Mexico and the Apalachicola River in a small town world famous for tupelo honey.

Truly a regional writer, North Florida is his beat.

In the early 90s, Michael became the youngest chaplain within the Florida Department of Corrections. For nearly a decade, he served as a contract, staff, then senior chaplain at three different facilities in the Panhandle of Florida—a unique experience that led to his first novel, 1997's critically acclaimed, POWER IN THE BLOOD. It was the first in a series of popular and celebrated novels featuring ex-cop turned prison chaplain, John Jordan. Of the John Jordan series, Michael Connelly says, "Michael Lister may be the author of the most unique series running in mystery fiction. It crackles with tension and authenticity," while Julia Spencer-Fleming adds, "Michael Lister writes one of the most ambitious and unusual crime fiction series going. See what crime fiction is capable of."

Michael also writes historical hard-boiled thrillers, such as THE BIG GOODBYE, THE BIG BEYOND, and THE BIG HELLO featuring Jimmy "Soldier" Riley, a PI in Panama City during World War II (www.SoldierMysteries.com). Ace Atkins calls the "Soldier" series "tough and violent with snappy dialogue and great atmosphere . . . a suspenseful, romantic and historic ride."

Michael Lister won his first Florida Book Award for his literary novel DOUBLE EXPOSURE. His second Florida Book Award was for his fifth John Jordan novel BLOOD SACRIFICE.

Michael also writes popular and highly praised columns on film and art and meaning and life that can be found at www.WrittenWordsRemain.com.

His nonfiction books include the "Meaning" series: THE MEANING OF LIFE, MEANING EVERY MOMENT, and THE MEANING OF LIFE IN MOVIES.

Lister's latest literary thrillers include DOUBLE EXPOSURE, THUNDER BEACH, BURNT OFFERINGS, SEPARATION ANXIETY, and A CERTAIN RETRIBUTION.

Thank you for reading BLOOD MOON!

And don't miss all the exciting John Jordan Mysteries in the BLOOD Series.

Be sure to visit www.MichaelLister.com for more about other John Jordan Mysteries and Michael Lister's other award-winning novels.

Join Michael Lister's Readers Group at www.MichaelLister.com to receive news, updates, special offers, and another book absolutely FREE!

CPSIA information can be obtained at www.ICGtesting.com
Printed in the USA
LVOW10s0923230815

451196LV00002B/13/P